DOCTOR WHO – TIME-FLIGHT

DOCTOR WHO
TIME FLIGHT

Based on the BBC television serial by Peter Grimwade by
arrangement with the British Broadcasting Corporation

PETER GRIMWADE

A TARGET BOOK

published by
the Paperback Division of
W. H. ALLEN & Co. Ltd

A Target Book
Published in 1983
By the Paperback Division of W.H. Allen & Co. Ltd
A Howard & Wyndham Company
44 Hill Street, London W1X 8LB

Phototypeset by Sunrise Setting, Torquay, Devon
Printed and bound in Great Britain by
Hunt Barnard Printing Ltd, Aylesbury, Bucks.

ISBN 0 426 19297 4

CONTENTS

1

Flight to Infinity

At 57,000 feet the air over the Atlantic was cold and clear. From the flight deck of Concorde Golf Victor Foxtrot, Captain Urquhart could see the curvature of the earth in a dark purple haze beyond the visor. For the passengers in the cabin, only the illuminated Machmeter gave any indication that they were hurtling towards London at over 1,300 miles an hour, twice the speed of sound.

Although British Airways flight 192 had left New York a mere two and half hours before, the journey was nearly over, as Captain Urquhart explained over the tannoy. 'Ladies and gentlemen, we'll be reaching our deceleration point in a few minutes and beginning our descent into London Heathrow'.

'Speedbird Concorde 192, you are clear to descend to flight level three seven zero.' The voice of air traffic control came through to the crew, giving them permission to leave their supersonic cruising altitude and join the queue of inbound subsonic aircraft waiting to land at Heathrow.

The First Officer, sitting on the right of the Captain, leant across to make an adjustment to the auto-throttle. Behind the First Officer, on the right of the narrow cockpit, the Flight Engineer scanned the myriad dials and gauges on the systems panel in front of him. For all three of them it was one of the most critical periods of the flight. Every ounce of their skill was needed to slow the aircraft until it was just subsonic at the moment of crossing the coast.

Captain Urquhart turned to his co-pilot with a smile of satisfaction. 'Mach 1.6. Sixty miles to subsonic point. We're spot on!'

Far away on the ground the progress of flight 192 was being followed on the radar screens in air traffic control. The voice of Captain Urquhart was heard over the radio. 'Speedbird Concorde 192. Level at three seven zero.'

The Controller gave further instructions. 'Speedbird Concorde 192, you are clear to continue descent to two eight zero.'

There was no reply from the incoming aircraft.

'Speedbird Concorde 192, will you acknowledge, please.'

A confused crescendo of atmospherics began to whistle in the Controller's headphones. For a moment he thought he could detect the Captain's voice beyond the interference. He transmitted again. 'Speedbird Concorde 192, will you acknowledge, please!'

But now there was only silence.

Suddenly the illuminated call sign on the radar which marked Concorde's progress started to flicker. Something was happening to the plane. The shimmering image on the tube grew fainter and fainter. Then it faded altogether from the screen. The Controller couldn't believe it. The aircraft had simply disappeared. He picked up a red telephone.

'Emergency. We've lost Concorde Golf Victor Foxtrot.'

8

Meanwhile, a vehicle of quite another kind was nearing London. But the TARDIS was not travelling in any air corridor known to Heathrow's flight controllers. Not that anyone on board really cared where they were going. They were far too upset. Adric had died in a desperate attempt to save the freighter hi-jacked by the Cybermen from crashing to the Earth. Tegan and Nyssa still could not come to terms with the loss of their companion.

'We can change what happened! We can materialise before Adric was killed!' Tegan pleaded with the Doctor.

'There are rules that cannot be broken, even with the TARDIS. Don't ever ask me to do anything like that again!' There was anger in the Doctor's voice. In their own grief Tegan and Nyssa had not realised how distressed he was at the death of his stowaway friend from Alzarius.

The Doctor spoke again, but more gently this time. 'You must accept that Adric is dead. His life wasn't wasted. He died, like his brother, trying to save others.'

As the Doctor recalled his adventure with the Marshmen in E-Space, Tegan and Nyssa came to understand how little they knew about the boy who had sacrificed his life, like his brother, Varsh, to save his friends.

Tegan was calmer now as she blinked back the tears. 'We used to fight, but I'll miss him.'

'So will I,' added Nyssa quietly.

The Doctor moved across to check the co-ordinates, and, sounding a great deal more cheerful than he felt, announced: 'A special treat. To cheer us all up!'

The two girls felt they owed it to the Doctor to put on a brave face. '1851. Earth. London.' Nyssa read out the intended time and destination. 'What's so special about that?'

'Hyde Park? The Crystal Palace?'

These clues meant nothing to someone from Traken, but Tegan realised at once that the Doctor was taking them to the Great Exhibition.

'Opening day?' suggested the Doctor. 'Pass the time of day with the foreign Royals?'

'Queen Victoria will not be amused,' thought Tegan to herself. 'Not if the Doctor's visit runs true to form.'

But the Doctor was already planning an afternoon's cricket at Lords. 'A few overs from Wisden and Pilch. I wonder if the Lion will be bowling ...'

'Let's get there first,' warned Tegan, who knew that when it came to reliability, the TARDIS was a poor second to any wonderful contraption they might find on display in the Crystal Palace.

'Nothing will go wrong this time,' promised the Doctor.

The words were still in his mouth when the control room began to shake and shudder.

'Nyssa, have you touched the dimensional stabilisers?' the Doctor shouted, darting to the controls.

'Of course not. All systems functioning normally.'

The vibration was clearly getting worse.

'Of course it could always be the relative drift compensator ... No.'

'Some sort of turbulence?' said Tegan with memories of a bad trip in her father's Cesna back home.

10

'Feedback from the zonal comparator,' the Doctor speculated, making frantic adjustments that did nothing to stop the TARDIS oscillating like a giant tuning fork.

'Another ship on the same space-time axis?'

'Another ship?'

It was a chance in a million. But Nyssa could just be right. In fact it could be the only explanation. The Doctor was already taking evasive action though neither Tegan nor Nyssa seemed to appreciate the danger. 'We're in the wash of another time-vehicle,' he shouted, trying to impress on them the seriousness of the problem. 'If we don't materialise it will destroy the TARDIS!'

2

An Unauthorised Police Box

At Heathrow, the sudden appearance on the radar of an unidentified object, on the flight path of the vanished Concorde, caused considerable excitement. The air traffic controller broadcast a general warning. 'Unidentified aircraft on approach to two eight left, will you acknowledge?'

To the controller's dismay there was an ominous silence.

The controller would have been more alarmed, a few moments later, had he been standing near the end of the airport's runway two eight left, when an out-of-date metropolitan police box appeared from nowhere and hovered a few hundred feet above the ground.

Inside the TARDIS all was calm again. The Doctor opened the scanner so they could admire the view of Hyde Park.

There was a sad irony in the fact that, while the Doctor's attempts to return Tegan to her place of work had always come to grief, now, as they turned to the screen, what they saw was no bird's-eye view of the Crystal Palace but a pilot's view of Heathrow.

'That's not Hyde Park. It's London Airport!' cried Tegan in alarm. 'I never thought I'd say it, but let's get out of here. We could be in the path of an incoming aircraft.'

Quite undismayed, the Doctor was already tinkering underneath the console. 'Co-ordinate override. Sort of anti-collision device,' he explained with that air of confidence Tegan and Nyssa had learned to distrust.

And if anyone was watching by the approach lights at the end of the runway, they wouldn't have been able to trust their own eyesight. As suddenly as it had appeared, the strange blue box was gone.

It had been a difficult day in Terminal One. A sudden fall of snow delayed several flights and more than the usual number of tired and irritated passengers were milling around the concourse.

A Terminal duty officer first saw the police box in the departure lounge. He had no idea how it could have got there, but he was quite sure it had no authorisation.

The duty officer wasn't the only one who knew the TARDIS had no business in the terminal building. Tegan was, for once, very conscious of being a stewardess, and didn't at all like the idea of explaining how she came to be, even partly, responsible for a police box at Heathrow. Thank goodness the Doctor had reset the co-ordinates. But she had reckoned without his sporting interests.

'Won't be a moment.'

'Doctor!'

Before they could stop him the Doctor was through the doors and off towards the airport bookstall.

Fearing the worst, Tegan and Nyssa peered from the TARDIS. The Doctor was coming back, totally engrossed in a copy of *The Times*.

'I don't know what English cricket is coming to.'

'Oh, Doctor!' chorused the girls in dismay, but from no concern for the Test eleven. The Doctor was being followed by a posse of Terminal officers and policemen.

'Are you responsible for this box, sir?' Andrews, the duty officer, was icily polite.

'I try to be,' bluffed the Doctor.

'Try to be is about it,' thought Tegan. And she hoped desperately than no-one would notice her uniform.

'Would you be so good as to open it, sir.'

'Is that a good idea?'

'I must insist, sir. Security.'

'Yes, of course. Security.'

'You have the key, sir?' Andrews was now a little more icy and a little less polite, and not to be put off by the Doctor's bluster.

'UNIT!' The Doctor produced the word like a rabbit from a hat. And indeed the effect was almost as magical.

'UNIT, sir?' Andrews was surprised the Doctor knew about the existence of the special security organisation. Tegan and Nyssa, who were unfamiliar with the Doctor's previous adventures on Earth and had certainly never heard of UNIT, took it for granted he was making it up. Though they had to admit, it was, even for the Doctor, an impressive performance.

'You'll do much better to check with department C19. Sir John Sudbury is the man you want.'

Suddenly the Doctor sounded a much more important person than the pompous man in the brown uniform. Tegan began to wonder if the Doctor really did have some connection with this UNIT set-up.

So did Andrews. 'And who exactly are you, sir?' he

said, trying not to be so cold and rather more courteous. It would do his career no good at all to upset a genuine UNIT agent.

'Just tell him it's the Doctor,' said the Doctor, as mysteriously as if he were James Bond himself. 'And do give my regards to Brigadier Lethbridge-Stewart. Unless, of course he's a General by now.'

Andrews turned away to radio his office.

The Doctor, feeling rather pleased with himself, grinned at Tegan and Nyssa. 'What did I tell you? We'll be away from here in a couple of shakes!'

Sir John Sudbury had other plans for the Doctor. The loss of a Concorde would be nothing short of a national disaster. That the Doctor should have turned up at this critical moment was the most amazing piece of good luck. If there was one person who could solve the mystery of the vanishing aircraft it was the owner of the police box in Terminal One.

Douglas Sheard, the Airport Controller, was less enthusiastic. For a moment he thought that the head of UNIT had taken leave of his senses.

'A Doctor with a police box? Really, Sir John ...' He spluttered into the telephone. With thirty million pounds of aircraft missing, not to mention the passengers and crew, he had more important things to do than worry about an unauthorised police box. But crisis or no, it would be very embarrassing to get on the wrong side of a man in Sir John's position. 'Of course, Sir John,' he oiled, 'I appreciate the political ramifications.' Just as well to humour the old boy and get on with the investigation in his own way. 'Surely, Sir John,' he continued, 'that's all the more reason for not wasting time with this Doctor.'

Sheard was surprised at the vigour of Sir John Sudbury's reply – after which there was nothing more to be said. 'Yes, I beg your pardon. If you insist.' He concluded as gracefully as he could manage, only to find Andrews from landside security waving a telex at him.

'The party with the police box in Terminal One have full security clearance from C19,' Andrews said, clearly amazed and peeved that the extraordinary young man should be given such a warm welcome by the top brass of UNIT.

'I've been talking to Sir John Sudbury. We are obliged to brief this Doctor on the disappearance of Victor Foxtrot,' Sheard explained, in a voice that no longer disguised his opinion of UNIT's interference.

'Good afternoon, gentlemen.' The Doctor breezed in with Nyssa and Tegan.

Sheard did not warm to the Doctor's appearance. Doctor, indeed! And as for his associates! A girl little older than his own daughter and a young woman in Air Australia uniform. Things had come to a pretty pass when he was obliged to discuss a major crisis with junior cabin staff. He shook the Doctor's hand, and turned his attention as politely as he could to Tegan. 'You're a stewardess.'

'Yes, that's right.' Had she not been so nervous, Tegan would have risen to a less gracious reply. But try explaining the Doctor and the TARDIS and Nyssa to the likes of the Airport Controller! And, if word got round, Air Australia might start asking some very awkward questions about why she had failed to report for duty. She pictured herself explaining Aunt Vanessa

17

and Logopolis and saving the universe from galloping entropy to that aggressive young personnel officer from Brisbane, and decided it was far better to stay with the Doctor, and get out of Heathrow fast. But the Doctor could never resist sticking his oar in, and here they 'were on the trail of a missing Concorde. Concorde? What on earth did the Doctor know about Concorde! She smiled at Sheard and hoped he would forget about her.

'I hear you're having problems?' The Doctor wanted all the details of the missing airliner.

Sheard introduced him to Clive Horton who had been on duty on air traffic control when the flight from New York was lost. The young man explained how, shortly after it had started the deceleration descent procedure, all trace of the supersonic airliner, known by its registration number as Golf Victor Foxtrot, faded from the radar screen. The experts in Sheard's office were unanimous that the event Horton had witnessed on the screen defied rational explanation. Flight 192 had not crashed. It had dissolved into space.

'Just like the TARDIS,' thought Tegan to herself. 'If only they knew!'

Listening to Clive Horton's report, the Doctor had spotted a rather interesting co-incidence. He turned to his companions. 'The turbulence in the TARDIS!'

'That forced us to materialise.'

'Cross-tracing on the time-space axis.' Nyssa was already thinking on the same lines as the Doctor.

'Exactly!'

The clever men from British Airways strained their ears, but it was so much double-Dutch to them.

'Do you know where the missing aircraft is?' By now

Sheard was desperate enough to listen to any theory that might throw light on the mystery.

The Doctor's answer, however, did little to reassure him.

'I suspect that it's not a question of where, but *when*!'

3

The Doctor Goes Supersonic

'Against my better judgement, I am obliged to do as you suggest, Doctor. But really! Why do you want us to send up another Concorde?' Sheard was under orders to follow the Doctor's instructions to the letter, but felt obliged to make a token protest at the man's fantastic notions.

The Doctor explained his plan yet again. 'We must follow the same route, same height, same speed. And, with my equipment on board, I can identify what I believe to be an exponential time contour.'

This was the second time the Doctor had advanced the idea of a time slip. On the first occasion Sheard pretended he hadn't heard. Now, out of self-respect, he felt obliged to challenge such unscientific nonsense. 'You really believe that Victor Foxtrot flew into ... a time warp?'

Not even Douglas Sheard's withering scepticism diminished the Doctor's self-confidence. 'Exactly. And you can't have a navigational hazard like that hanging about the galaxy.'

Sheard counted slowly to ten. The man was obviously a lunatic. All the same, if it ever got out that the Airport Controller had co-operated in this madcap scheme, he would be the laughing stock of the whole airline industry. He was saved from further speculation by a phone call from the control tower. Glad at least to see the back of the Doctor and his companions, Sheard passed on the information. 'Golf Alpha Charlie is ready for boarding.'

The operations office was buzzing with rumours of the missing Concorde when Captain Stapley and his co-pilot, Andrew Bilton, were ordered to prepare Golf Alpha Charlie for take-off.

As they crossed the tarmac to the waiting aircraft, Captain Stapley explained the briefing. 'This scientist wants to take up some special equipment to monitor the approach used by Victor Foxtrot when she went through the deceleration phase.'

'Morning, Skipper. All ready for loading.' Flight Engineer Roger Scobie called cheerfully from the cabin door as they reached the aircraft steps. There was something more sardonic than usual about the way Roger was grinning.

'Is the gear on its way?' asked the Captain.

'Coming over now.' Roger pointed to the maintenance hanger.

Pilot and co-pilot both turned to look. A fork-lift truck was making its way towards the plane. Lying on its side on the loading platform was the Doctor's TARDIS.

The Doctor, Tegan and Nyssa followed the TARDIS in an airport car.

In her travels with the Doctor, Tegan had seen many remarkable things, but as she stepped out of the car onto the hard-packed snow and looked up at Concorde she caught her breath. The aeroplane dazzled in the sunshine, brighter than the frost. She saw why it was so

22

often compared to a bird – a wild creature of the upper air, with graceful swept-back wings, but, for all its power, a thing tamed to the use of man. With its lowered visor and long, elegant legs, it looked a touchingly submissive beast, patiently waiting for its master to arrive, and command it to soar to the borders of space.

The Doctor led the way up the steps. As they entered the cabin they were met by Captain Stapley, who introduced the two young men on the flight deck behind him.

'Would you all go back and get strapped in for take-off,' he asked them, and returned to his place in the cockpit to complete the pre-flight checks.

Nothing was said by Stapley, Bilton or Scobie as they taxied out to the holding point, apart from the routine calls and checks. But the same thought was uppermost in their minds. This was the wierdest bunch of punters they had ever flown – to say nothing of the police box in the cargo hold.

'Golf Alpha Charlie. Right turn there. After the Trident departs. Line up and hold, two eight left.'
   'Golf Alpha Charlie. Roger.'
   'Speedbird Golf Alpha Charlie. Cleared for take-off. Surface wind is two nine zero, twenty knots.'
   'Speedbird Golf Alpha Charlie. Cleared for take-off.'
   'Okay. Ready to go then? Three, two, one, now!'
   'Airspeed building.'
   'One hundred knots.'
   'Power checked.'
   'V one.'
   'Rotate.'

Every eye on the airport turned to the runway as the great bird reared up and lifted itself into the air.

'You seriously believe Victor Foxtrot went into some sort of time slip?'

The Doctor had joined the crew on the flight deck and was sitting in the jump seat behind Captain Stapley, who was finding the idea of the time contour as difficult to swallow as had Douglas Sheard.

'It's the logical explanation.'

'Sounds a pretty rum idea to me.'

'Hang on a moment, Doctor.' Roger Scobie turned from the engineer's panel with a mischievous gleam in his eye. 'If we follow Victor Foxtrot's course and end up somewhere over the rainbow – well, we're on a one-way ticket, just like Captain Urquhart's lot!' Roger had no doubt they would be back on chocks at Heathrow within the hour and had posed the problem out of sheer devilment.

'You're forgetting the TARDIS,' replied the Doctor gravely.

'The TARDIS?' said Captain Stapley. 'You mean that police box?'

'That's right,' said the Doctor, and left the flight deck feeling just a little wounded by their mocking smiles.

The TARDIS, which had caused such mirth at the Doctor's expense, was meanwhile lying on its side in the narrow baggage hold of the aircraft. Together with Nyssa and Tegan, the Doctor lowered himself from a trap door in the main cabin to the confines of the cargo compartment.

'That's odd,' he muttered scornfully, 'this plane's smaller on the inside than it is on the outside.' He was still a little aggrieved by the crew's lack of confidence in the police box onto which he was now clambering.

It was not the Doctor's habit to enter the control room through the ceiling, but with the TARDIS stowed sideways on, the doors were now uppermost. The Doctor lowered himself towards the console and fumbled for the switch that would bring the auto-gravity system into circuit. Suddenly the whole room rotated through ninety degrees, bringing the floor back where it belonged. Tegan and Nyssa came running in.

'So useful when you want to maintain a dignified attitude.' The Doctor grinned, delighted to show of the TARDIS's versatility.

The Doctor got to his feet and activated a panel of instruments on the side of the console. It was crucial to monitor exactly what happened in the next few minutes, when Concorde began her descent deceleration procedure.

Concorde Golf Alpha Charlie was also being monitored in air traffic control, where Douglas Sheard had joined Clive Horton to keep a very close eye on the Doctor's test flight.

'Alpha Charlie is now at 58,000 feet, one hundred and fifty miles off the Cornish coast. Scheduled to turn on its approach any minute now,' Clive explained.

'Speedbird Concorde Golf Alpha Charlie.' Captain Stapley came in clear and confident over the radio. 'Now at six north, thirty west. Request permission to return to London.'

'Golf Alpha Charlie. Clear to turn to port. Route via

Sierra November, fifteen west to London.'

'Roger. Golf Alpha Charlie. Turning to port.'

Clive turned to the Airport Controller. 'They're now on the same configuration as Golf Victor Foxtrot.'

Sheard nodded. Everything was normal. The whole operation was a waste of time and money and had got them nowhere.

The first thing the Airport Controller noticed to indicate that it was not quite as straightforward as that was the look of alarm on Clive Horton's face. Then he too heard the whistling interference on the radio.

'It's happening again!'

'Speedbird Concorde Golf Alpha Charlie ...'

For a moment they could make out the voice of Captain Stapley through the ringing atmospherics. Then it was submerged in the same unearthly noise that Clive had heard the day before.

'Golf Alpha Charlie. Do you read?' Clive Horton called over the air in vain.

Sheard's eyes were riveted on the radar screen. The blip that showed the progress of Alpha Charlie was starting to flicker. They were losing the aircraft's transponder signal. Horrified, the two men watched as the cluster of glowing numerals grew fainter and fainter, then vanished altogether.

'Doctor, we're time-travelling!' Nyssa had been watching the dials on the TARDIS console with the Doctor.

'But the column isn't moving,' protested Tegan.

The Doctor nodded. It was all happening as he had expected. 'Concorde has just flown into the time contour!'

26

The Captain and his crew on the flight deck had no idea of the dismay at Heathrow, or the excitement in the TARDIS, as the Doctor's theories began to be proved right. All their navigational instruments indicated they were making a normal approach to London Airport. The only sign of any unusual activity was the radiation meter.

Captain Stapley watched the needle flickering in the alert section. 'Must be a solar flare.' One or two other Concorde pilots had noted this phenomenon, though it had never been serious enough to abandon the cruise climb.

'I doubt it,' interrupted the Doctor, reappearing on the flight deck. 'It's reacting to centuries of galactic radiation through which we're passing.'

But Stapley no longer took the Doctor seriously. He turned his attention to air traffic control. 'Speedbird Concorde Golf Alpha Charlie. Permission to descend to three seven zero.'

To his surprise, London was silent. He called again. 'Golf Alpha Charlie. Do you read?'

'I'm afraid your radio is useless, Captain. By my calculation we're the spatial equivalent of four hundred billion miles from air traffic control.'

Captain Stapley flashed the Doctor a look that was almost hostile. Loss of radio contact was a serious problem and the Doctor was no help at all, going on about this time-warp nonsense. But, for all his rationalis-ation, he felt a surge of dread, as if he were close to something alien and unknown. He prayed for a simple explanation.

'Golf Alpha Charlie. Descend to three seven zero.'

The relief of the crew at the voice on the radio was

considerable. But it was nothing to the surprise of the Doctor.

Captain Stapley turned and smiled. 'Would you like to put your seatbelt on, Doctor. By *my* calculations we're twenty minutes from touch-down.'

The familiar smell of kerosene greeted them as they walked down the aircraft steps.

'I ought to feel at home, getting in and out of airplanes,' thought Tegan, as she looked round the airport scene. 'But everything seems so unreal after the TARDIS.'

'There's something very unreal about all of this.' Nyssa felt an intuitive sense of unease.

The Doctor felt acutely embarrassed. They had no right to be back at Heathrow. But how could he explain that to Captain Stapley?

Prompted by Nyssa's observation, he started to recite to himself:

'That's why this tree
Doth continue to be,
Since observed by yours faithfully, God.'

'What's that, Doctor?' the Captain asked in a friendly voice. He was now quite sorry for the Doctor. After all, the poor man had come back with a lot of egg on his face.

'"To be is to be perceived",' the Doctor quoted back. 'A naive eighteenth-century philosophy.'

At this point, something very strange happened to Nyssa. For a moment she saw the airport around her as a reflection in a window. Against her conscious will, the focus of her eyes was drawn through the glass to a frightening vortex beyond. There were bodies,

28

cadaverous shapes – putrid, rotting, utterly horrible. She screamed.

As the others rushed round to comfort her, the spectre was gone. She tried to explain what she had seen.

'There's nothing there,' said Andrew Bilton reassuringly.

It all started to make sense to the Doctor. He should have realised. They were under the influence of more than a time contour. 'Perceptual induction,' he muttered to himself.

'What are you talking about, Doctor?' Andrew had heard enough nonsense for one day.

'I want you to concentrate very hard,' the Doctor replied with renewed urgency in his voice.

Roger Scobie was not impressed. 'You don't give up, do you, Doctor!'

'Concentrate! Look at everything! Observe it in every detail!' There was something about the Doctor now that commanded their attention. 'Concentrate! All together! It must be a concerted effort!'

Captain Stapely shivered. Pure imagination, of course, but ever since that bit of bother during the deceleration he had sensed a certain atmosphere. Perhaps the Doctor wasn't such a fool as he appeared.

They all felt the temperature drop. From nowhere a moaning wind blew up.

Tegan was staring at a Pan Am jumbo jet. It rippled and twisted like a mirage in the desert. 'That plane! I can't focus properly!'

It was true for all of them. The whole world was reducing to an image from a half-forgotten dream.

'What are you doing to us!' shouted Captain Stapley.

'Perceptual induction. And I'm *undoing* it,' insisted the Doctor. 'Keep concentrating. It's the only way to fight it and find out where we really are!'

The Doctor was in deadly earnest. They were battling with a powerful unseen force.

'But we're at Heathrow!' interjected Stapley, desperately trying to reason away the invading unknown.

But the Doctor was giving no quarter. 'You *think* you're at Heathrow. So did I – well almost – up to a moment ago. But now I know this isn't Heathrow at all. And you're beginning to have your doubts!'

They were cold now and desperately afraid. But the Doctor continued, ruthlessly, to exploit their will power.

'Can't you see the coherence breaking up!'

All around them, layer upon layer of what they had taken to be Heathrow was peeling away to reveal an infinite void. The wind rose to a hurricane. The whole air screamed. The airport ripped apart, as if it had been nothing but a painted cloth.

Then there was darkness.

4

The Coming of the Plasmatons

It was a wilderness. A cold, primordial tract of land, that rolled away, flat and empty to the horizon.

The Doctor came to his senses first. Then the others, one by one, struggled to their feet, dazed and confused.

'Where are we?' stammered Captain Stapley.

'I think you were right first time, Captain.'

'Heathrow?' He was numb with shock.

'Some one hundred and forty million years ago.'

It was all too much for Roger Scobie. 'I think I'm dreaming,' was all he could say.

'Quite the reverse, Mr Scobie,' the Doctor corrected him. 'You've just woken up.'

'I don't believe it!' Andrew Bilton gazed round the solitary place.

The Doctor had no such credibility problems. 'Definitely Jurassic,' he decided, looking at the forbidding terrain. 'There's a nip in the air though, so we can't be far off the Pleistocene era.'

'The ice age?'

The Doctor nodded. 'You know, it's at times like this I wish I still had my scarf. Better watch out for the odd brontosaurus,' he added casually – an observation that did nothing to restore the shattered morale of Captain Stapley and his crew.

'Were they the creatures I saw?' asked Nyssa, still

fearful of her horrifying clairvoyance.

'I doubt it,' replied the Doctor. 'Though I suspect what you saw was from this time zone.'

Captain Stapley was struggling to make sense of what had happened. He had to concede that the Doctor's hypothesis fitted the facts. 'Do you really mean we've gone backwards down this time contour?'

'Have you any other explanation?'

Captain Stapley had not.

But Andrew Bilton was still clutching at straws. 'We were on Concorde,' he protested, hoping that everything else was just a bad dream.

At the mention of Concorde, another thought struck the Captain. 'How did we land on *this*?'

They could see Golf Alpha Charlie parked at the end of a fortuitously long stretch of level ground, possibly a dried out mudflat, toughened by the encroaching cold.

The crew took one look at the long ribbon of tyre tracks and broke out in a cold sweat. Without knowing it, they had just crash-landed a hundred tons of supersonic aircraft.

The Doctor agreed they were lucky to be alive.

'The touch-down was perfect!' Andrew's memory of the landing just didn't square with what must have been an impact such as he had only previously experienced on the simulator.

'Like having a tooth out under hypnosis,' explained the Doctor. 'You don't feel a thing.'

Captain Stapley shared his co-pilot's perfect recall of a normal approach and landing. 'The descent into Heathrow was utterly real,' he protested.

'So was the Indian rope trick,' remarked the Doctor.

It occurred to Stapley that the same thing must have

happened to Captain Urquhart as he brought in Flight 192 the previous day, no doubt believing they were making a normal let-down into London. The passengers and crew could be anywhere in this wasteland, and, without the Doctor's help, totally at the mercy of an unbelievably potent hallucinogenic force.

'We shall find them,' the Doctor reassured him. 'Let's hope no one finds *us* first,' he added, a little less optimistically. 'Behind most illusions there's a conjuror. And in this case you can be sure he's not gone to all this trouble for our entertainment.'

They all noticed the anxiety in his voice.

'Doctor!' Tegan pointed. From where she was standing she had caught sight of the other Concorde, previously hidden behind an outcrop of rock. Perched further along the mudflat, Victor Foxtrot looked like some prehistoric animal, entirely at home in this pristine landscape. Tegan was already away to have a closer look.

'Tegan! Wait!' But she seemed not to hear the Doctor calling.

Tegan suddenly stopped running. 'Look!'

As he caught up with her the Doctor followed her eyeline to the horizon.

'A building!' she exclaimed. 'Or are we hallucinating?'

'I don't think so. The illusion is always one of normality.'

'Well, that's not exactly Terminal Three.'

Dominating the skyline was a large pyramid of dark stone.

'But who could have built it!'

No accident of nature had produced this megalithic fortress. Neither, in this prehistoric desolation, could it be the work of any man.

As they cautiously moved forward, something caught the Doctor's eye, in a shallow crater to one side. It was an enormous skeleton, though not of any living thing.

'I think the answer might be over there.'

'A spacecraft?' asked Tegan.

The Doctor walked into the crater to get a better view of the wreckage. Looters or salvagers had long since stripped it bare. The wind and freezing rain had eroded the gaunt superstructure. But it was undoubtedly the hulk of a vast ship.

Nyssa felt a sudden jab of fear. Something was gnawing at the threshold of her mind. Surprised at her own spontaneity, she cried out. 'Danger! We must follow the Doctor!'

She moved instinctively towards the second Concorde. Andrew, Roger and the Captain had no choice but to follow her. Yet when they came to the brow of the hill the Doctor and Tegan could not be seen.

A band of mist obscured the horizon. As they peered into the haze it seemed to evaporate. Out of the barren tundra a four-lane motorway, surging with traffic, stretched ahead, as far as the eye could see.

'It's the M4,' cried Roger.

'It's an illusion,' warned Nyssa.

'It might lead us out of this time warp,' replied Andrew, stepping forward with Roger towards the beguiling vista of civilisation.

'Bilton! Scobie! Stay where you are! And that's an order.' Captain Stapley had learned from the Doctor. Like Nyssa, he wasn't to be taken in by this phantom reality. 'Remember the Indian rope trick.'

The two officers remembered Heathrow that was not Heathrow. With renewed scepticism they outstared the vision. The view of tarmac and traffic faded. They were alone in the wilderness. Once again they had been the victims of some form of group hypnosis, like the spectators of the Indian mesmerist. They must be on their guard against another attack.

'What was the Indian rope trick?' asked Nyssa who knew nothing of that curious tale of the Raj. How, in front of all the sahibs and memsahibs, the fakir threw his rope up into the air, climbed up, and vanished. And how only a photograph had shown the truth – no magic, no gateway to heaven ...

'Just the rope lying on the ground, and this Indian juju man and his oppo behind the bushes, laughing like a couple of skunks.' Roger finished the story.

'Get down!' Captain Stapley had seen something.

A group of men and women came into view, trundling a large heavy object. Nyssa was appalled. Somehow these people had got hold of the TARDIS.

Roger and Andrew were more interested in the task force itself.

'There's Dave Culshaw and Angela Clifford!'

'They were on Victor Foxtrot!'

They had found some of Captain Urquhart's passengers and crew. Co-pilot and engineer were already half-way to joining their colleagues. Captain Stapley could do nothing to hold them back.

Andrew was the first to reach the young stewardess. 'Angela!'

The girl recognised him at once, obviously delighted. 'Andrew! You didn't tell me you had a New York Stopover.'

'What are you talking about?'

'See you in the bar in half an hour.'

He realised that this little band, in their Savile Row suits and airline uniforms, were blind to the alien landscape, and knew nothing of the strange labour they were required to perform. They day-dreamed normality.

'Look, old chap. This is all a bit of a snare and a delusion ...' Roger was having the same trouble with Captain Urquhart's co-pilot.

'Do you fancy that new Indonesian restaurant?' Angela was looking forward to an evening out in Manhattan with the man who was frantically trying to drag her back to reality. But the spell could not be broken.

'We'll have to grab them!'

The struggle was viewed from a distance by Captain Stapley and Nyssa. The Captain was on the point of going to help his two crew members when Nyssa saw the cloud.

Stapley had experienced a tornado once in Arizona, and he was reminded of it as the great tongue of white fire came whirling in and hovered over Bilton and Scobie. It grew in size, seeming to draw its substance from the air.

The white mass divided into seven hideously bland seething conglomerates which transmogrified into creatures; faceless dead things dragged to life.

Andrew and Roger had seen the invaders. They turned to defend themselves. Encircling them, the seven grey transmutes linked their spavined limbs to contain the two men. As their unnatural flesh touched, it merged again, oozing and bleeding, until the seven members were reabsorbed into each other.

Bilton and Scobie were now hopelessly engorged in the trembling matter, like solids digesting in the gut of an animal. Then, as swiftly as it had come, the huge globule rose up and was gone.

Bilton and Scobie had disappeared.

5

The Magic of Kalid

'Sheraz, sheraz, tumal baloor ...' The thin, strangulated voice that chanted these arcane words could have been that of a muezzin summoning the faithful to prayer. But it was no holy man who stood before the great crystal ball in the sombre heart of the Citadel that the Doctor and Tegan had seen on the horizon, and the power that Kalid called forth was as dark as the granite walls of the chamber where he practised his magic arts.

The Doctor was right to fear such a man as this; for Kalid was no ordinary conjuror.

He was no ordinary man either, with his yellow oriental face, bloated like the body of a drowned dog and gangrenous with age and excess, with broken teeth and rotting gums that contorted his mouth into a permanent leer. His height too, for a Chinaman – if that was his race – was remarkable, and his girth, concealed by a bright coat of damask, as monstrous as the force he invoked.

'Sheraz, sheraz, tumaal ...' Kalid called again and the crystal clouded. He gazed in the swirling mists and saw the Doctor and Tegan wandering back from the ruined spaceship. He was pleased with the power at his command. He could see all things; and all things obeyed his will.

'Verram, verram, xeraak namaan ...' He would show his power to this Doctor.

The Doctor meanwhile, had returned to a very frightened Captain Stapley.

'Those *creatures*!' The Captain had no words to describe the emanations that he had seen spirit away his two crew members. 'They just took off with Bilton and Scobie!'

The Doctor's first thought was that Stapley had been hallucinating again. But Nyssa, who was much less susceptible, was as upset as the Captain by what had just happened.

If any doubt remained in the Doctor's mind as to the reality of what Captain Stapley and Nyssa had just witnessed, it was about to be dispelled.

As the voice of Kalid echoed in the darkness of the Citadel, another cloud appeared. The Doctor saw the horror on the faces of Tegan and the Captain.

'Behind you, Doctor!' hissed Stapley.

The Doctor had no time even to turn and face the horrid eviscerations that had formed behind him. He was instantly absorbed into the shapeless mass.

The Doctor felt like a drowning man who has gone under for the third time. He knew there was no point in struggling. In fact, there was a strange calm at the centre of the agglomeration.

He could hear a murmuring, like the distant roar of the sea in a conch shell. It was almost as if a giant had woken from a deep sleep and was trying to whisper some great confidence. Was it his imagination, or could he hear someone or something calling out to him?

'Doctor ... Doctor ... Help ... Help!'

There was no doubt about it. Some unknown intelligence was trying to communicate.

'Help us, Doctor!' The voice was growing stronger and more desperate. 'Beware ... beware the renegade! Help!' The voice grew incoherent as if terrified at its own revelation.

'Stop!'

Captain Stapley and Tegan turned from their efforts to free the Doctor to face Nyssa who was watching their exertions with a faraway look on her face.

'You mustn't fight it!' Although she couldn't herself hear the distant voices, she just *knew* the Doctor wasn't in danger.

And in the Citadel, Kalid, who saw everything in the crystal sphere, knew that he must release the Doctor before the voices betrayed him.

'Evaneragh!' he cried out.

'What's happening now?' Tegan could suddenly see the shadow of the Doctor inside the cocoon.

As quickly as it had materialised, the substance dissolved and evaporated, leaving the Doctor, looking rather surprised, on the ground.

Stapley rushed forward to help him. The Doctor smiled reassuringly. 'Captain Stapley, are you all right?'

'Am *I* all right!' The Captain was amazed at the sheer nerve of the man.

The Doctor got to his feet and dusted himself down.

'Those were the creatures that got hold of Bilton and Scobie!'

'What creatures?'

'Those blobs!'

'You mean the Plasmatons?'

'Is that what you call them?'

'Protein agglomeration.' The Doctor was casually matter of fact. 'Random particles assembled from the atmosphere. Quite inanimate I assure you.'

Captain Stapley had twice, now, seen the Plasmatons, and in his opinion they were highly animate. He considered the Doctor's eccentric explanation dangerously inadequate. 'But, Doctor,' he protested, 'there's no technique that could create matter like that, out of thin air!'

'Isn't there?' The Doctor instantly countered his objection. 'What about the energy that telepathically generated the illusion we were at Heathrow! Do you think that can't operate on a physical level?'

Captain Stapley shook his head and wondered for a moment if he was in a madhouse.

'Doctor!' Nyssa interrupted. She had something far more serious to recount than a visit from the Plasmatons. But no one was listening.

'Simply a form of psychokinesis,' the Doctor continued.

'You mean that spoon-bending nonsense?'

'Doctor!' Nyssa tried once more to prise into their conversation. 'Those people were taking away the TARDIS!'

The Doctor's shock at the theft of the TARDIS was equalled only by Kalid's joy as the great box was trundled into his chamber by the impressed workforce of airline passengers that Nyssa and Stapley had spotted leaving the Concorde.

'You have your work. Go to it!' Kalid dismissed his labourers.

As the bemused business executives and cabin staff wandered out of the chamber, Kalid moved eagerly towards the TARDIS. He had seen it before in the crystal and longed for the moment when it would be his. He stretched out a jaundiced hand to the door.

It was locked.

'Didn't you even bother to see where they were taking it?' The Doctor was appalled they had let the TARDIS be removed so easily.

Rather unreasonable of him, thought Stapley, seeing how Bilton and Scobie had weighed in, only to be abducted by those Plasmaton things.

But Nyssa and Tegan understood the Doctor's concern only too well. Without the TARDIS they were stranded.

They were not, however, alone.

A man was running behind a line of rocks on the high ground above where Captain Stapley, Tegan, Nyssa and the Doctor were discussing what to do next. He dropped to his knees behind the cover of a large boulder, breathing heavily. Such exertion did not come easily to a man of his years. After a few moments he began to get his breath back. He brushed at the mud on his tweed suit and hauled himself up to a position from where he could observe the people in the valley below him. There were four of them. They didn't seem familiar from the New York flight. But one of them was in uniform. Plenty of gold braid. A pilot perhaps from

43

the second aircraft he had just seen. He resisted the impulse to join them immediately; they too might be contaminated. But he couldn't survive, let alone escape from this place, on his own. He would have to make contact.

'Hey!'

The Doctor and his companions looked towards the skyline from where a rather distinguished, bearded figure was walking slowly towards them.

Not a word was spoken until the newcomer was within a few yards of Captain Stapley.

'Are you from the other Concorde?' The man spoke warily.

'Captain Stapley, British Airways.' Stapley held out his hand.

The stranger continued to regard them with deep suspicion. 'Professor Hayter, University of Darlington.' He grudgingly offered the information like a card player forced to reveal his hand.

'You must be from 192! Where are all the other passengers? What happened to you?'

Professor Hayter was reassured by the Captain's brisk questioning. 'You're not hallucinating?' He sounded desperately hopeful.

'Certainly not.'

The Professor relaxed. 'You've no idea what it's been like resisting alone.'

He turned his attention to the Doctor and the two girls. What was Captain Stapley doing with such an unlikely rescue party!

The Doctor guessed what he was thinking. 'Don't worry, you're not imagining us.' He introduced the others.

Professor Hayter nodded. He still didn't know what to make of them.

Captain Stapley appreciated how he must feel about this improbable trio. He quickly explained how, if it hadn't been for the Doctor, they would never have tracked down the missing Concorde.

Hayter found this hard to believe, but at least help, in some form, had got through. 'How did the Russians let you land?' he asked eagerly.

'The Russians?' The Captain had no idea what the Professor was talking about.

'Aren't we beyond the Iron Curtain?'

Stapley wished they really were in the USSR. It would be far easier to escape from the Soviet Union than from the far end of a time contour.

'This must be Siberia,' the old man insisted.

'Well, not exactly.'

They would have a hard time explaining the truth to Professor Hayter.

Kalid turned from the crystal sphere. The Plasmaton mass had entered his chamber. The organic shroud dissolved and dispersed, revealing Bilton and Scobie.

'You will return to your work.' Kalid studied their reaction to his command. Thanks to the interference of the Doctor, these two men had learned to resist the illusions.

The co-pilot and engineer began to walk somnambulantly from the chamber. Kalid smiled; all was well. They had forgotten all the Doctor's advice.

Suddenly, from the corner of his eye, Bilton caught sight of the TARDIS. Something stirred in his memory. He moved across to the police box. 'TARDIS

45

... TARDIS ...' The word sprang from some far recess of his mind. What it meant he had no idea. 'TARDIS?' But that was just an old police box. And then he remembered the Doctor. Of course! The TARDIS! He became aware of the dark, cold room, from the corner of which a shadowy figure was watching his every move. 'Rope!' He remembered something else. 'Rope trick!' That was it. It all came flooding back. He had been hallucinating again.

'Ram sharaa, Inoora xuror,' Kalid began to chant. The young officer could not be allowed to resist the power.

Bilton felt himself losing his momentary hold on reality. He felt dizzy and anxious.

Then he felt perfectly well again. It was a normal day at Heathrow.

'You will return to your work.' Kalid spoke once more.

'Speedbird Concorde 193, clear for take-off.' A normal working day, and Andrew Bilton was flying to New York ...

The Doctor was impressed by Professor Hayter's ability to resist the perceptual induction. His resilience was soon accounted for.

'Hypnosis is my special subject at Darlington,' Hayter explained. 'So I was able to contra-suggest.'

Alone among the passengers of the crew of the first Concorde to slip into the time contour, the Professor had been aware that they were the focus of a powerful hallucinogenic force, although even he had momentarily lost consciousness during what he still insisted on calling 'the hi-jack'. But the old man had

46

obviously had quite a battle to keep control of his own mind. 'Hyperstimulation of eidetic images,' he explained. 'The most powerful hallucinatory induction I've ever come across. They must be using ultra-sonics.'

'Who are they?' the Doctor interrupted.

'I don't know. Even the guards are disguised.'

'The guards? You mean the Plasmatons?'

'The what?'

'Never mind,' said the Doctor. There was no time for explanations, particularly with a man like Professor Hayter. That was the trouble with scientists; they were so narrow-minded. For the moment the Doctor needed Hayter to show him where his fellow passengers had been taken.

The Professor was most reluctant to return to the prison from which he had just escaped.

'You're not serious,' he protested, as the Doctor outlined his plan.

'Hayter, I've got to find my crew and the crew and passengers from 192,' insisted Captain Stapley. He sympathised with the old man's fears, but he had a duty to make sure everyone escaped.

'And I've got to find the TARDIS,' added the Doctor.

'TARDIS?' It was not a word in Professor Hayter's vocabulary.

The Doctor did not elucidate. A discussion with the Professor on time and relativity would get them nowhere.

Tegan, as usual, was less discreet. 'Without the TARDIS we'll never get back to the twentieth century,' she blurted out.

'What did you say?' The scientist from Darlington reacted with depressing predictability.

Before the Doctor could change the subject, Nyssa had chipped in. 'She's absolutely right. We've all travelled a hundred and fifty million years down a time contour.'

The Professor didn't bat an eyelid. 'You're both hallucinating!' He dismissed the two girls' explanation.

Tegan obstinately continued with her account of how the 192 had been snared in a time warp. But the Professor was having none of it.

'Unless we get them away from here, this could turn into dementia praecox.' He spoke with the grave authority of a true expert.

The Doctor said nothing. He needed to keep the old boy's confidence; Professor Hayter could lead them to the TARDIS.

'Professor, there's no time to explain.' Captain Stapley was equally pragmatic. 'I need you to show me where I can find the others. And the Doctor has got to get back his ...' He faltered. Let the Doctor convince the old man about the time warp. 'The Doctor must retrieve his equipment,' he concluded with neat circumlocution.

'If you insist, Captain,' Hayter conceded rather ungraciously. 'The prison centre is somewhere on the other side of that hill.'

The little party moved off down the valley. Their breath misted in the cold air and their footsteps crackled on the frosty earth. They instinctively moved fast to keep warm, though everyone kept a wary eye open for a return of the Plasmatons.

As they progressed, Professor Hayter gravitated to the side of Captain Stapely. He felt he could trust the Concorde pilot. He was not so sure about the Doctor, however. The world was full of Doctors with woefully inadequate qualifications; there were several at his own university. 'What is this equipment of the Doctor's?' he asked suspiciously.

Captain Stapley felt like a schoolboy. He couldn't explain how Golf Alpha Charlie had been used to transport an old police box without making himself sound a complete idiot. 'It's a TARDIS,' he said, with confidence he did not feel.

Professor Hayter signalled them to halt at the end of the valley. On the horizon they saw the great pyramid that Tegan and the Doctor had spotted on their earlier exploration. That was where the TARDIS must have been taken, thought the Doctor. With a bit of luck the Professor could show them the way in without drawing attention to themselves.

'How did *that* get built in this wilderness?' said Captain Stapley, gazing at the Citadel on the horizon.

'Slave labour I expect,' said Professor Hayter bitterly.

The Captain was just wondering how they would ever convince the Professor they weren't in Russia, when Nyssa cried out: 'Doctor!'

She was rigid with fright and fighting for breath.

'Something's happening ... I can't ...' She could hardly mouth the words.

'No!' she screamed, as if trying to ward off an invisible invader.

'It's the radiation,' shouted the Professor. 'I said we

49

should keep away from this place.'

'Keep still!' The Doctor waved back Stapley and Tegan who had moved to Nyssa's help.

They watched Nyssa carefully. She was suddenly calmer.

'Do not approach the Citadel!' Her voice was deep and resonant and seemed to belong to another person altogether. 'Return to your ship ... There is great danger.'

The Doctor studied Nyssa for a few moments in silence, then spoke as if she were a stranger. 'Who are you?' he asked.

'What's happening?' whispered Captain Stapley, overwhelmed by the sudden transformation of Nyssa's personality.

'The intelligence is using Nyssa as a medium,' explained the Doctor.

'Hysteria triggered by ultra-sonics,' sneered the Professor contemptuously, dismissing the Doctor's observations with his own diagnosis.

'Be quiet!' The Doctor turned back to Nyssa. 'Who are you?' he repeated. 'What do you want?'

'Krishnan, krishnan ...' Kalid could see everything in the crystal ball. He had silenced the voices in the Plasmaton mass around the Doctor; now he must silence this girl whose mind was attuned to the Great One.

'Krishnan, krishnan xaraa ...'

Nyssa groaned, feeling pain and despair that were not her own. 'We are ... we are ...' She felt another force that froze the words in her mouth. 'The control divides

50

us ...' A dual power struggled for supremacy of her consciousness. 'The control shall be resisted,' the unknown voice uttered again. 'There is so little time. You must resist ...'

'Veraam, veraam, xarak namaan!' screamed Kalid inside the Citadel.

'Look!' shouted Tegan. 'It's happening again!'

They all looked up. The Plasmaton cloud had formed in the sky above them. It hovered for a moment, a whirling tongue of white fire, over Nyssa, then slowly descended and swaddled her. She stared out helplessly from the blubbery cage.

'A bioplasmic shield,' observed the Doctor. 'Somebody wanted to stop her talking,' he added more ominously.

'We've got to get away from here,' muttered Hayter, noting that the enemy had more than psychological weapons at its disposal.

'We've got to get Nyssa out of *there*,' said Stapley. But for all his bravery there was nothing he could to to prise the bonded matter apart.

'I'm afraid we don't have the right kind of energy,' said the Doctor.

'We can't just leave her!'

'We must find the source of the power.' The Doctor looked towards the Citadel.

'You go on, Doctor. I'll stay with Nyssa,' urged Stapley.

Tegan, however, knew that the Captain was far more useful helping the Doctor track down the TARDIS. 'I'll stay with Nyssa,' she insisted.

Hayter was near panic with all this talk going on. 'Continuing to the Citadel is madness!' he cried.

'If we don't get the TARDIS back, we'll be trapped here for ever!' Tegan gave the Professor short shrift for his lack of spirit.

The Doctor agreed with Tegan. 'If Nyssa gets free you are both to go back to the Concorde.'

'You bet!'

'Come on, Captain, Professor.'

Professor Hayter couldn't believe such stupidity. 'Don't you realise the effect will only get worse as we near the centre of the radiation!'

Stapley looked at the Professor in disgust.

The Doctor expressed the Captain's feelings precisely. 'Is that a reason for abandoning your fellow passengers!'

There was no sign of any activity as they neared the Citadel.

While they walked, Captain Stapely thought about what had just happened to Nyssa. He turned to the Doctor. 'If the intelligence was trying to communicate with us, who was trying to stop it?'

That was just what the Doctor was wondering. 'Something with the same resource of psychokinetic energy,' he suggested.

'Another intelligence?'

The Doctor nodded. Captain Stapley could well be right.

6

The Doctor and the Magician

'Shamorsherah ... shamorsherom ...'

Though the Doctor and his companions had met with no opposition as they entered the Citadel, Kalid, who saw all things, could observe their approach in the miasmic images that formed and re-formed in the crystal sphere. His face twisted in a horrid smile. Soon they would all be in his power.

The Citadel was a cold, unfriendly place. The dark stone corridors were like tunnels excavated from the bedrock. They crossed and twisted alarmingly. It was as well that Professor Hayter had such an excellent sense of direction.

They advanced deeper and deeper into the Citadel; there was still no sign of anybody.

'The place is deserted,' whispered Captain Stapley.

'Don't you believe it,' answered the Professor. 'Those guards appear from nowhere.'

'Those guards, as you call them,' said the Doctor, 'are fully occupied looking after Nyssa.'

Neither Professor Hayter nor Captain Stapley had any idea what he was talking about.

The Doctor tried to explain. 'Those creatures you saw were particles of protoplasm bonded by psychic energy. The essential protoplasm can take any form.'

'Such as the shield round Nyssa.' Captain Stapley now saw exactly what the Doctor meant.

'Yes. But I suspect that the power and the raw material is limited. So as long as Nyssa is protected ...'

'No Plasmatons!' said Stapley, jumping to the same conclusion as the Doctor.

Professor Hayter wondered why the Captain took such egregious nonsense seriously. The Doctor was a crank.

'I've never heard such an extravagant explanation,' he snorted derisively.

Captain Stapley was irritated by the Professor's reflex scepticism. Granted the strange forces at work in the place, what the Doctor said made good sense. 'Then how do you explain what happened to Nyssa?' he challenged the old man.

It was really beneath Professor Hayter's dignity to contribute to such an unscientific debate, but that ridiculous young man needed putting in his place.

'Some form of projection. Maybe part hallucination,' he suggested airily. 'Scientifically speaking ...'

But the Doctor cut him short. 'Scientifically speaking, I'd like you to show me where we can find the others.'

Nyssa felt no fear. There was a womb-like peace within the shield. She could dimly see the face of Tegan, peering forward like an eager child – nose against the glass of a toyshop window.

'Can you hear me?' Tegan mouthed. 'Are you all right?'

But Nyssa was a world apart.

54

'Nyssa … Nyssa …' The voice that came to her was inside the shield itself. 'Resistance … resistance,' it pleaded. 'Kalid shall be resisted!'

'Who are you?' asked Nyssa.

It grew brighter as they turned the corner and saw the end of the tunnel. Captain Stapley led the way forward. Hugging the walls, they tiptoed towards the source of the light.

The corridor ended in a great hall from which radiated several other passages. In the centre of the hall was a large rotunda, forming a room within a room, constructed with much greater precision and of smoother blocks than the surrounding walls.

A large group of men and women were chiselling with crude implements at the tight mesh of stones which concealed the inner room.

'There's Bilton and Scobie!' The Captain had spotted his crew members, mindlessly labouring with the crew and passengers from the 192.

The Doctor's first thought was that Andrew and Roger could lead them to the hiding place of the TARDIS. But he didn't need Professor Hayter to tell him that they had lapsed into a deep, though active, state of trance. It would be quicker to look for it himself. He started to walk round the circular hall.

'If we could separate Bilton and Scobie …' began Stapley, thinking aloud that it would be relatively easy to bring his co-pilot and engineer to their senses and, with their help, work on the others.

'Look out for the guards,' cautioned the Professor, who was not a man for heroic gestures.

The Captain tried to reassure him. 'If the Doctor's

theory is right ...' He looked round. 'Where is the Doctor?'

The Doctor had vanished.

It was the tracks of some heavily loaded sledge or barrow that brought the Doctor into one of the side corridors. If the grooves on the floor had indeed been left by the TARDIS, he needed only to follow the tramlines to the terminal ...

One corridor led to another and intersected a third. The Doctor kept going. He finally came to an archway in which was set a door of stone. Some hidden mechanism swung aside the heavy portal, and the Doctor stepped into Kalid's chamber.

At first he saw nothing of the pedestal in the centre of the room, or the great globe of crystal which rested on it, or the necromantic trappings around the walls. His eyes went straight to the far corner of the chamber – and the TARDIS. He hurried over to it.

'So you are here at last, Doctor.'

The Doctor spun round. The sinister magician had stepped from the shadows behind him.

Captain Stapley walked right round the rotunda inside the great hall looking anxiously for the Doctor.

The Professor bore the Doctor's disappearance with more equanimity. 'I don't know what this Doctor's qualifications are,' – he adopted a tone of voice heard frequently in the senior common room of Darlington University – 'but if you ask me, the man's a lunatic.'

'I don't believe I did,' said Captain Stapley.

The passengers and the Concorde crews toiled away at the side of the circular inner room, like marauding insects assailing the walls of a giant hive. It was a strange sight. Blue-rinsed American matrons, a pop star and his manager, financiers, stewards from the airline: they all applied themselves, without thought of protest, to the interstices of the blocks, uncaring of the debris that rained on their smart clothes.

They took no notice either of Captain Stapley or Professor Hayter.

Stapley watched them in amazement. 'What do you think's behind that wall?' he asked the Professor.

'Another wall, I shouldn't wonder. It's called hard labour.'

The Captain sighed. He started to explain. 'The Doctor's theory is that it's a hi-jack in time rather than space ...'

The professorial features contracted into a sneer.

'This isn't the Soviet Union, Professor,' the Captain battled on. 'The Doctor ...'

'This Doctor needs his head examined,' announced Professor Hayter.

The Doctor stood between Kalid and the TARDIS. 'So you're the conjuror?' he finally spoke.

'I am Kalid,' the oriental replied grandly.

'You say that as if you expected a round of applause.' The Doctor answered with a lack of respect that obviously displeased the magician.

'Have a care, Doctor. You are not summoned to my domain to play the clown.'

'Your domain?' The Doctor's flippant tone changed to one of assumed interest.

'Here Kalid rules!'

'Then I apologise for my levity.' The Doctor bowed

with exaggerated politeness. Kalid, however, failed to spot the irony of the gesture and inclined his head in return. 'Not to mention my curiosity,' added the Doctor, hoping for some sort of explanation.

'What troubles your mind?'

'What you're doing in this time zone for a start.'

'Shall Kalid not travel where the spirit leads him?'

The Doctor was silent for a moment. He glanced round the chamber before turning back to Kalid. 'Would the spirit have anything to do with the ruin of that spaceship outside the Citadel?'

There was no response to the Doctor's probing.

'Spaceship?' asked Kalid blandly.

'Yes,' said the Doctor, unconvinced by the other's assumed ignorance.

'Space is within us,' Kalid persisted enigmatically.

'Then how exactly do you travel?'

'By the power of the Great One.' Kalid narrowed his eyes. 'In the deserts of Arabia I learned all the magic arts.'

The Doctor had had enough of this play-acting. 'Seven league boots, eh? Magic carpet? I suppose it makes for convenience.' He jeered at the artful pomposity of the grotesque figure before him.

Kalid's anger was very real. 'You mock me, Doctor!' His sunken eyes burned like live coals and he uttered a terrible warning. 'Do not doubt that I could summon furies and cacodaemons, a company of cherubim, or Lucifer himself!'

The Doctor knew this was no idle threat. 'Yes, you're surrounded by a lot of powerful bioenergetics,' he agreed. But there was more – or perhaps less – to Kalid than that. 'I can't help feeling, Kalid,' he continued 'that there's something a great deal more mechanistic about all this.'

'Mechanistic?' Again the innocence.

'What are you doing sitting at the end of a time contour, like a spider in a web? And what do you want with my TARDIS?'

Kalid smiled. 'My familiar spirits have told me of your miraculous cabinet. The spirits have told me you would come.'

'Your spirits are certainly well informed,' said the Doctor, irritated by the inscrutability of the man.

'I hold the whole genius of Night bound to my will,' Kalid ranted on, puffing himself up like a great toad. 'And now the Great Elemental has summoned *you*, Doctor. Destiny has brought you to me.' He continued to talk in riddles.

'But not just me, Kalid.' The Doctor was determined to get some sense out of him. 'What do you want with all those passengers?'

'Slaves are required in my domain.'

'You have the Plasmatons.'

'They have other uses.'

Just as the Doctor thought: the power that controlled those manifestations was limited.

'You mean you need that psychotronic energy for something else!' The Doctor was thinking of Nyssa trapped in the bioplasmic shield.

'The power must be used for the great work we shall do together.'

'We?' The Doctor had no intention of co-operating with this inflated poseur.

'Together we shall scourge the entirety of time and space!' proclaimed Kalid.

The Doctor had heard it all so many times before. These vainglorious tyrants with their dreams of absolute power. 'You can exclude me from your wizardry,' he replied sharply.

But Kalid was not offering the Doctor any choice. 'You cannot resist, Doctor. In this place all things obey Kalid. Come!' He led the Doctor to the crystal in the centre of the room, and began to chant. 'Vizaan, vizaan, zanoor minaz ...'

The crystal clouded. Out of the mists appeared the image of Tegan and Nyssa.

'You see your friends?'

He called a second time: 'Vizaan! Vizaan!'

The mists rolled back. When the crystal cleared again the Doctor could see the great hall and rotunda.

'Your Captain Stapley and his fellow mortals.'

The Doctor was very impressed at such a display of clairvoyance. But such power could not come from a mere human being. The incantation was releasing energy from elsewhere.

'You're not in control here,' the Doctor challenged Kalid. 'You're as mortal as anybody else!'

7

The Enemy Unmasked

Captain Stapley and the Professor had no idea that the Doctor could see them — albeit fleetingly in the crystal ball.

The Captain would have appreciated a sighting of the Doctor. He wished the man wouldn't just wander off like that.

Hayter, his confidence boosted by the prolonged absence of the guards, was all for making contact with Bilton and Scobie and shepherding the passengers back to the relative safety of the aircraft. 'Your crew are in front of you,' he urged Captain Stapley. 'Or do you have to ask the Doctor's permission first!'

'Don't provoke me,' growled Stapley. But it did seem a little lacking in initiative not to try and rescue his two officers.

Hayter and Stapley walked up to the group attacking the rotunda. Hayter selected the young stewardess Andrew Bilton had originally recognised in the party with the TARDIS. Stapley approached his First Officer.

'Andrew!'

'Hello, Skipper.' Andrew Bilton was very matter of fact, totally convinced that the man beside him was sitting in the left-hand seat on the flight deck, preparing to take off. 'I've got the Met. report. We'll clear those thunder storms by the time we get to the subsonic cruise.' He was absorbed in a waking dream in which he acted out the routine of ordinary life.

'Andrew!' Stapley tried to shake some sense into him.

Angela Clifford, the stewardess, saw Professor Hayter as a particularly obstreperous passenger. But she was trained to deal with the likes of him. 'Will you please sit down, sir, and fasten your seat belt. We're about to take off.'

'Listen to me!'

'The bar will be open as soon as we're airborne,' she retorted in her most cut-glass accent.

'Andrew!' said the Captain. 'We're not on Concorde. Remember the Doctor!'

But nothing seemed to convince the First Officer he wasn't at Heathrow, about to leave for New York.

'Oxygen checked. Flight control inverters on. Anti-stall system on ...' He launched into the pre-flight checks.

To his horror, Captain Stapley felt himself being drawn into Andrew Bilton's fantasy.

'Altimeters checked. Navigation radios set ...'

'Stop it, Andrew!'

But the Captain could already hear the whine of engines, and the ghostly outline of the flight deck was taking shape around him. 'We must fight ...' he stammered, forcing his conscious mind to hold back the illusion.

But the hypnotic rhythm of the calls only stimulated the hallucination.

'Brakes.'

'Checked,' responded the Captain, half-believing he

really was in the pilot's seat.

'Throttles.'

'Idle.'

'Throttle masters.'

'On.'

Stapley made another desperate attempt to hold back the images flooding up from his subconscious. 'We must fight ...' But the dream was becoming its own reality. 'Speedbird Concorde 193 to tower. Permission to start engines ...' He made one more supreme effort. 'Professor!'

Hayter rushed to the Captain's help. 'Wake up, man!' The Professor pulled him away from Andrew Bilton. 'Concentrate! What about the Doctor, Captain Stapley!'.

'The Doctor?' Stapley blinked. His perception reverted like a change of shot in a film. His mind was in control again. 'The Doctor! And my crew!' He was angry with himself for losing control. It wouldn't happen again. 'Bilton!' He turned back to his co-pilot with renewed determination. 'Mr Bilton, remember what happened at Heathrow!'

'What's that, Skipper?'

'Remember the Doctor. And Nyssa. And Tegan. Remember Tegan?'

The mention of the pretty Australian stewardess seemed to have a positive, though unexpected effect. 'Rope,' he muttered.

'Rope?' said Captain Stapley.

But the Professor knew they were winning. 'You've triggered a rational association,' he cried to the Captain. To Andrew Bilton he spoke gently but persistently. 'That's it! Rope, rope, rope ...'

'The Indian rope trick!' exclaimed Bilton. He blinked, and looked around in amazement at the bizarre activity in the great hall.

'Together with your box, the power will be absolute,' shrieked Kalid. 'We shall command the whole universe!' he climaxed in a manic falsetto.

'I've always found domination such an unattractive prospect,' replied the Doctor, concealing his disgust in urbane understatement.

'Shall I be forced to compel you, Doctor,' said Kalid quietly, with the reassuring charm of a rattlesnake.

'There is no power that will give you control over the TARDIS!'

Kalid's body stiffened.

The Doctor thought the sorcerer was about to attack him. Then he realised the man was in some sort of pain.

Kalid moved swiftly to the crystal. Of course. Part of his mind was on another plain. Like a wild animal, he felt danger.

The Doctor looked over Kalid's shoulder. In the nebula he could see the great hall where Stapley, Andrew Bilton and the Professor, like a group of subversive pickets, were persuading the passengers to down tools.

Kalid was angry. He chanted urgently. 'Shiraaz shiraaz kazaan ...'

As if a door had opened, chilling the room, the Doctor felt the flux of energy.

'Shiraa, shiraa, kazaan ...'

The Doctor watched helplessly as Plasmaton shapes formed in the hall. The amorphous things soon engorged the rebels.

'Iznamin ... Iznamin ...' The crisis over, Kalid's voice was soft and coaxing.

But the danger had been great enough to impress his servitors; which meant, thought the Doctor, that Nyssa would now be free. At least the two girls would be safe in the plane.

The suddenness with which the shield evaporated, voiding Nyssa on the ground, took Tegan by surprise.

'Nyssa! Are you all right?' She knelt beside her fellow companion.

'Of course.'

'What happened!'

Tegan's question was rhetorical, but Nyssa answered confidently. 'The power dissolved. It was needed elsewhere.'

'What are you talking about?'

'I don't know.' She was as surprised as Tegan at her sudden intuitions.

'I promised the Doctor we would go back to Concorde.

'No!' The same oracular voice.

'But, Nyssa ...'

'We must go to the Citadel!' Some dreadful imperative urged her forward.

'We'll only get caught.'

Nyssa shivered. 'The Doctor's in danger!' she gasped – then gave a cry: 'Kalid!'

'Eevaneraagh!' cried out Kalid, as the Plasmaton cumulation entered his chamber.

The massive discharge of energy as the protoplasmic matter unbonded was quite terrifying in the enclosed space, like an explosion of steam from a boiler. In seconds, all trace of the Plasmatons was gone, leaving Hayter and the Concorde crew on the floor.

Captain Stapley was the first to his feet, delighted to see the Doctor. Then they all became aware of the extravagant figure that stood beside them.

'Who is this man?' asked Professor Hayter.

'The oriental gentleman calls himself Kalid,' said the Doctor.

Captain Stapley turned indignantly on the magician. 'Are you responsible for the abduction of the Concorde passengers and crew?'

'Is it you who authorised mass hallucination?' challenged the Professor.

Kalid regarded them all with leering disdain. 'Your questions are irrelevant.'

'I don't think so.' The Captain stepped aggressively towards him. Bilton and Scobie moved in alongside, confident now that they faced a tangible enemy.

'No!' cautioned the Doctor.

'Sheraz aazoor,' hissed Kalid.

The air shimmered. The three officers stopped dead as if they had walked into a plate-glass window.

'What's happening?'

'He's thrown up a barrier. I did try and warn you.'

Kalid turned away from his would-be assailants. He had some unfinished business with the Doctor. 'I require the TARDIS,' he announced unequivocally.

'You're wasting your time, Kalid.'

Kalid said nothing. His evil face inclined towards his captives; he knew how to put pressure on the Doctor.

But the menacing smile soon froze on his lips. His pockmarked features spasmed with pain. He pressed a hand to his temple, and moved to the crystal where he began a desperate chant.

'Arogogorah abrao abelatha ...'

The Doctor crept up behind Kalid so that he too could see into the crystal ball. He was surprised at the cause of Kalid's discomforture.

Tegan and Nyssa had entered the Citadel.

Tegan wished heartily they had done what the Doctor said and gone back to Concorde. She was ill at ease in this dark and sinister place.

'But where are we going? she asked Nyssa as they walked down the gloomy corridor.

'To help the Doctor.'

'Is this your intuition again?'

'Yes. Can't you feel it too?'

'No!'

'We must find the centre.' Nyssa was strangely confident. Her sense of authority disturbed Tegan. 'Trust me,' she added, aware of her companion's anxiety.

But Nyssa's inspired sense of direction appeared to have brought them into a cul-de-sac.

'It's a dead end,' said Tegan, running her hand over the bland rock face that barred their way.

'We must continue.' Nyssa moved resolutely forward.

To Tegan's amazement the wall opened up, revealing a narrow passage beyond.

The two girls passed through the divide.

Kalid was appalled. "Not even I have dared penetrate the heart of the Citadel!' he gasped.

'You mean you've not been *able* to!' cried the Doctor, encouraged by the evidence that there was a force not entirely under Kalid's control.

'The power must prevent all mortal advance,' protested Kalid.

But the Doctor knew that a greater power protected Tegan and Nyssa and urged them forward.

'You will watch them suffer for this!' Kalid screamed at the Doctor, and began a demonic incantation.

Tegan and Nyssa heard nothing of Kalid's vile litany, although they both sensed the invisible eddy and flow of mighty forces. But there would be no turning back; their progress was inexorable.

The young boy who stepped out of the shadows to bar their way was a timid unthreatening figure. But he stopped the two girls in their tracks.

'Adric!' gasped Tegan in disbelief, as she gazed at their brave friend who had sacrificed his life to prevent the destruction of Earth by the Cybermen.

'No! Adric's dead!' But for all her steely assurance, Nyssa was disturbed by the presence of the pale wraith in front of them.

'Go back, or you will destroy me.' The boy spoke with immeasurable sadness.

Grief, uncertainty, longing conflicted with the resolution of the girls. But despite the distress she felt at this sudden confrontation, Nyssa knew that their old companion existed merely in their shared imagination. 'It's the only power Kalid has left to stop us,' she whispered.

'How can we be sure?' Tegan was in an agony of indecision. Her doubts were instantly exploited.

'Go back, or you will destroy me,' pleaded the boy.

Tegan dared not move forward, terrified lest a miraculously ressurected Adric should die a second death.

The young man turned to Nyssa who was plucking up courage to continue. 'If you advance you will kill me, Nyssa.'

'We can't take that risk!' Tegan had grabbed Nyssa's arm.

Nyssa didn't know what to do. Then she saw the badge. 'Adric's wearing his badge!' she cried.

'It was shattered when the Doctor destroyed the Cyber Leader.'

'Exactly!'

'Come on!'

Sure now of his unreality, Tegan and Nyssa closed in on Adric. The boy watched them accusingly. They reached out their hands to thrust him aside, only to feel the empty air.

There was an unnatural scream and Adric vanished.

Shaken but undeterred they continued.

The girls needed all their courage as more nightmare emanations, drawn from the dark of their own minds, surprised them. But neither Melkur from Traken nor a roaring Terileptil could stop them.

They continued. All sense of time and space abandoned them. The unknown centre drew them towards itself like a lodestone.

There was another barrier. They waited before it like two postulants.

Groaning as if it were a living thing, the stone split apart. A cold luminance whitened their faces.

They stepped forward into the light.

'They have entered the Sanctum!' Kalid could no longer see the girls in the crystal. He trembled with rage. Nyssa and Tegan had been granted access to the centre of the power while he, Kalid, must remain at a distance.

He turned away from the sphere. 'Doctor, you will give me the key of the TARDIS!' He was desperate now.

The Doctor shook his head.

'Then you will see your friends destroyed and you yourself annihilated!'

The Doctor stood his ground. 'I don't think so,' he answered defiantly. 'We've all got rather good at resisting your sorcery.'

'You will not resist my combatant!' There was something ominously convincing about Kalid's voice. 'Sotou monduru, sotous abraou, phil thao thiaf!' The diabolical invocation summoned the very essence of darkness.

A thin skein of ectoplasm formed in the air. As Kalid continued his evil mantra, the hovering matter dilated.

Unperturbed, Captain Stapley seized a metal rod. 'Just a ball of cotton wool.'

'I'm not so sure,' cautioned the Doctor. There was something frighteningly different about this new manifestation.

As the metal in Stapley's hand impacted with the nascent shape there was an explosion. The Captain felt as if a thousand volts coursed through his body. He staggered back towards Bilton and Scobie.

'Kalid is drawing on deeper reserves of power,' warned the Doctor. 'That thing is bonding itself into something far more dangerous than a Plasmaton!'

The writing intumescence grew larger and larger. It bifurcated. At the end of each trunk a serpent's head appeared: a head with eyes, mouth, fangs and forked tongue. Each mouth hissed like a whole pit full of vipers.

'Well, Doctor?'

'The answer is still no, Kalid.'

'The TARDIS key, Doctor!'

The hissing expanded to a roar. Bilton, Scobie, Stapley and the Professor cowered in the corner as the beast lunged.

'Do you really want to see your friends die!' shouted Kalid, above the bellowing of the creature and the cries of the terrified men.

Only a gentle moaning disturbed the calm of the Sanctum. Tegan and Nyssa trod softly as if on holy ground. They looked round, awed and curious.

They had penetrated a small circular chamber, in the centre of which was a large open sarcophagus.

Nyssa knew what was required of her. Placed against the side of the room was an array of unearthly minerals. She prised off a huge chunk of the alien rock. 'Help me,' she called to Tegan, surprised at its unreasonable weight. 'We must act. The Doctor ...' She staggered towards the sarcophagus.

'What are you doing?' shouted Tegan.

With a vigour that belied her frail body, Nyssa swung back the rock and hurled it into the centre of the sarcophagus.

There was a massive explosion which threw both Tegan and Nyssa senseless to the ground.

The monster twisted its torso upwards for the kill. But

even as its fetid jaws parted, the reverberation reached them from the Sanctum.

A rushing wind surged through the chamber. The beast gave an agonising roar. Kalid recoiled against the wall, screaming with pain and tearing at his body.

The creature that had terrorised them crumpled like a paper dragon. Within seconds it was gone without trace.

'Look at Kalid!'

They turned to where the magician was lying in the corner, his flesh draining to liquefaction.

The Doctor was amazed. Kalid must have been a Plasmaton all the time.

'There's got to be a perfectly simple, orthodox explanation.' The Professor was tired of this masquerade. He delved into the pedestal beneath the crystal ball. 'Bioenergetic powers indeed ...' he muttered to himself. 'Intellectual garbage!'

'You won't find anything,' said the Doctor wearily.

'Won't I!' the Professor positively squawked with triumph.

As the others gathered round he pulled out modules and circuit boards. 'Psychotronics was it?' He turned maliciously to the Doctor. 'I call this *electronics*!' He dropped an armful of components on the floor.

'I don't understand.' The Doctor stared, nonplussed.

Across the room something stirred.

'No, Doctor. You never do understand.' A voice came from the shadows.

There was something alive inside Kalid's diaphanous robe. Like a pupating beetle it tore itself free from the cloth.

A dark and ominously familiar figure stood up. 'You never do!'

It was the Master.

8

The Power in the Sanctum

'As gullible as ever, my dear Doctor.' The Master's eyes gleamed with exultation. The incursion into the Sanctum had been a setback which cost him his disguise, but he had humiliated his rival. Very shortly, using the Doctor's TARDIS, he would penetrate the power centre himself.

'So you *did* escape from Castrovalva.' The Doctor confronted his old enemy. 'I should have guessed.'

But there was never a moment when the Doctor suspected the prosthetic persona of Kalid concealed the evil Time Lord. Nor could he imagine how the Master had gained control of the unseen power that maintained his disguise in the same way as it controlled the Plasmatons.

'How you love the company of fools.' The Master was watching Hayter dismember the apparatus beneath the crystal ball. Neither the Professor nor the crew had any great interest in the meeting of the two arch adversaries.

For a brief moment Professor Hayter held the stage. 'Magic, as in lantern,' he lectured. 'Sophisticated and terrifying, I do not dispute ...'

'Hang on a moment, Professor!' Flight Engineer Scobie, who knew a great deal more about electronics than Professor Hayter, had been examining the centrepiece of the chamber. He turned to the Professor like a recalcitrant student. 'This crystal,' he objected. 'There's no connection, no radio link ...'

The Doctor joined them. 'That crystal is just a point of focus. The communication is purely telepathic.'

'Then what's all this equipment for?' snapped the indomitably sceptical old man.

'What indeed!' said the Doctor, examining with mounting excitement the bits and pieces Hayter had removed. He turned back to the Master. 'These components are from your TARDIS!'

The Master was looking less pleased with himself. The Doctor felt his self-confidence returning as he realised the Master's predicament. 'You're stranded here,' he went on. 'That time contour was a desperate lifeline to the future.'

The Master did not deny it. His eyes narrowed. He spoke softly; he was chillingly polite. 'I need your TARDIS to penetrate the Sanctum.'

Another piece of the jigsaw fell into place. The Master needed the power in the Sanctum as a new energy source for his own time machine. The Doctor wondered again what kind of power it could be. Perhaps the Master would reveal the information. 'I think you might be too late,' he said provocatively. 'The power seems to have expended itself.'

The Master quickly put him right. 'The recuperation will be swift. Your companions have disturbed the neuronic nucleus ...' His face twisted with pleasure. 'But they will have paid for that incursion with their lives.'

There was consternation amongst the young crew members. The Doctor fought back a feeling of panic with the ruthless logic of his own observations.

'Tegan and Nyssa are as likely to have been protected as destroyed,' he assured the others. 'The power works against you as well as for you,' he reminded the Master.

The Master knew this only too well. It was the reason for his anxiety and haste. He needed the force under his total control. 'The key, Doctor.' He raised the Tissue Compression Eliminator.

The black, twig-like thing with its bulbous end didn't frighten Bilton and Scobie. They stepped forward to defend the Doctor.

The Doctor knew better. 'No heroics, gentlemen,' he interposed. 'The Master will eliminate you without a second thought.' He placed the TARDIS key in the black-gloved hand of the Master.

'Very wise, Doctor.' The Master went straight to the TARDIS.

No one, except the Doctor, had spotted the old police box in the corner of the chamber.

'Good heavens!' exclaimed Professor Hayter. 'That's never the TARDIS.'

'Unfortunately, it is,' the Master deplored as he opened the door. 'So typical of the Doctor's predilection for the third rate.'

It was beyond the Professor's comprehension that grown men should play out an hysterical charade, such as they had just witnessed, for the possession of a telephone booth. He appealed to the Doctor. 'What does the man want with an obsolete Metropolitan …'

A whirring and a groaning sound filled the air, unfamiliar to all present save the Doctor.

Professor Hayter froze.

The TARDIS dematerialised.

The Professor's lips moved silently like an elderly goldfish that has just been fed. He finally articulated: 'We're hallucinating.'

Captain Stapley was equally surprised, but he knew when to believe the evidence of his own eyes. 'Is that how you travel, Doctor!'

The Doctor smiled. 'Not exactly the first-class end of the market, but a serviceable vehicle, Captain Stapley.'

Professor Hayter was still in shock. 'Some kind of miasma,' he stammered weakly.

The Doctor had had enough of this sour-faced Doubting Thomas. 'I do not wish to believe, therefore I hallucinate,' He rounded on the Professor. 'Is that your philosophy of Darlington Man?'

'What we've just seen isn't possible,' Hayter protested.

'Try explaining that when the Master materialises in the Sanctum.'

'Have you any idea where this Sanctum is?' asked Captain Stapley.

The Doctor wished he had. He might even be able to get there first.

Then Bilton remembered the wall that he and the passengers had been trying to demolish.

'Could be it,' said the Doctor.

But, as the Captain pointed out, it was odd that the Master should need brute force to unseal the hidden room. Why couldn't he walk in like Tegan and Nyssa?

The Doctor thought he understood. 'The power source is unstable,' he explained. 'One moment it works for the Master, the next against.'

It was time for the Doctor to take up the work started

by the Master, and force his way into the rotunda in the great hall. He rejected the assistance of the Concorde crew since he doubted whether they would be able to resist the hallucinogenic radiation so near the power source. Captain Stapley was a little put out, however, when the Doctor decided to ask Professor Hayter to accompany him.

'The Profesor has shown formidable resistance,' he explained. 'Are you game?' he asked the old man.

Hayter had said nothing since the Doctor had attacked his academic integrity. His mind was in a turmoil. If this amazing young man was not, after all, a charlatan, then a lifetime's research had just been stood on its head. But suppose there *was* an entirely unknown dimension? He would publish a paper. There would be honorary degrees, lecture tours ...

'Professor?'

They were all looking at him. He smiled. 'Certainly, Doctor. Glad to be of help.'

'By the way.' A thought occurred to the Doctor as they were leaving. 'If the Master turns up again, don't be surprised. It may take him a little time to discover I left the co-ordinate overdrive switched in.'

The Doctor and Professor Hayter hurried down the corridor towards the great hall. The Professor chuckled. He had been thinking of his fellow passengers, toiling at the wall like Egyptian slaves. 'I'll say one thing, Doctor. For some of them it'll be the first honest day's work they've done in their lives ... Even if they do think they're bent wood hatstands,' he added spitefully.

The great hall, when the Doctor and the Professor

arrived, looked more like an airport during a strike of baggage handlers. Confused and angry passengers wandered helplessly around, the more militant amongst them demanding to know what was going on from anyone in uniform.

'Doctor, they've stopped hallucinating!' cried Hayter.

'That's not necessarily a good thing,' muttered the Doctor, as they heard the angry buzz of protest from Concorde's first-class passengers.'Are you good at explanations, Professor?'

Angela Clifford, the young stewardess, saw the Professor arrive with the stranger. She extricated herself from an overweight Milwaukee computer salesman who was telling her what he thought of British Airways In-Transit arrangements, and hurried across.

'This is the Doctor,' said Professor Hayter, neatly passing the buck. 'He's come to help us.'

Quickly establishing that the passengers were in good shape, the Doctor moved on to address the motley assembly, now close to mutiny, that were gathered around the rotunda. Keeping his account of the unlikely situation as simple as possible, the Doctor did his best to convince the stranded travellers that their only hope of a return to civilisation lay in a determined assault on the already half-demolished wall of the inner room.

The ladies and gentlemen of flight 192 were not an easy lot to convince, but through Professor Hayter's authority – developed from years of bullying on departmental committees – and the Doctor's charismatic charm, they were finally persuaded that a desperate situation required a desperate remedy.

They started work.

'It's incredible,' said Angela to Professor Hayter, as she watched the passengers, who so recently had been enjoying the luxury of Concorde, labour at the stonework like navvies. 'How could we do all this without realising it!'

Hayter did his best to explain the hallucinatory power, the source of which they would soon discover on the other side of the wall.

'Won't that be dangerous? What if the force returns?'

'Fight it!'

'How?'

'Focus your mind on something you're very sure of. Your family. Fish and chips ...'

Professor Hayter was thoroughly enjoying himself as he explained his own techniques of contra-suggestive resistance. Never, in the laboratory at Darlington, would he be able to conduct an experiment on this scale. 'Come on everybody!' he said turning his attention to the workforce. 'We haven't much time.'

The unlikely stonemasons were making good progress.

'Nearly there, Doctor! Doctor?'

The Doctor, as usual, had wandered off. A Corinthian pillar at the far end of the hall had drawn his attention.

'The Master's TARDIS!' he exclaimed as the Professor joined him.

'That pillar?'

'Of course, that's where he's hidden the other passengers.'

Hayter gulped. 'It's not big enough!'

'Something else for me to explain later,' said the Doctor casually.

The Professor's spine tingled. 'That revolutionises the whole concept of relative dimension!' He all but genuflected in front of the Doctor. 'Oh Doctor, if only I were a younger man and had the time to make use of your knowledge.'

'Time? That's another thing,' replied the Doctor tantalisingly.

Worlds within worlds, universes beyond the known universe kaleidoscoped in the Professor's mind. He was dizzy with excitement.

But something else had attracted the Doctor's attention. 'What's this?'

A cable snaked out of the half-open door of the Master's TARDIS.

'I want to see where this goes.'

He followed the trail. It soon became clear that the trunking encircled the rotunda. Various components were connected at regular intervals.

'An induction loop!' cried the Doctor. 'So that's how he generated the time contour!'

Hayter looked at him, desperate now to understand more of the Doctor's amazing technology.

'Don't you see what this means?'

'I certainly do not,' said the Professor who would have given his pension to know the half of it.

A terrible new urgency entered the Doctor's voice. 'The Master's already harnessing the power in the loop. The Sanctum!'

He dashed back to where Angela was acting as unofficial site foreman on the demolition of the rotunda wall. The Professor, who could hardly wait for a peep into the Master's TARDIS, followed reluctantly.

'We've got to get that wall down at once!' the Doctor shouted. 'Tegan and Nyssa are behind it!'

In Kalid's chamber Scobie was investigating the apparatus beneath the crystal ball. He was totally at sea with the outlandish components.

The return of the Master was heralded by the same whirring they had heard when the police box first vanished.

'Quickly!' shouted Captain Stapley, and he pushed Roger Scobie and Andrew Bilton into a dark recess.

The three men had hardly recovered from the further amazement of watching the TARDIS reappear when the Master opened the door and stormed towards the pedestal in the centre of the chamber.

Like a car thief, indignant that his stolen vehicle has broken down on him, the Master fretted and fumed as he sorted various circuit boards from his own TARDIS. How typical of the Doctor to travel in a machine that was unserviced, unsafe, and light years out of date!

'I've got an idea,' whispered Captain Stapley. 'Roger, you wait here for the Doctor. Andrew, you come with me.'

Stapley and Bilton tiptoed across the chamber, right behind the Master's back, and into the Doctor's TARDIS.

As Bilton and Stapley walked through the double doors into the TARDIS control room they staggered to a halt, stunned with the disbelief of any stranger who enters the time machine that something could be larger inside than out.

'I don't believe it,' said Andrew Bilton.

But wonder was a luxury they could ill afford. They had, possibly, only seconds before the Master returned.

'You're never going to try and take off!' Andrew was watching the Captain as he scrutinised the instruments on the console.

'Of course not. But somewhere there must be a control for those doors.'

'We lock the Master out of the TARDIS?'

'Maybe not out of the TARDIS, but at least we can keep him off the flight deck.' Stapley looked round, daunted at the array of unfamiliar dials and switches. 'Always assuming this *is* the flight deck.'

The Captain selected a control at random. 'Here goes.'

Only a buzzing resulted from Captain Stapley's intervention. He tinkered recklessly with more levers and buttons.

Andrew Bilton watched him anxiously. 'I hope you know what you're doing, Skipper.'

'Not the remotest.'

A sudden whir swung them round to face the screen which had opened with a view of the Master still at work in the chamber.

'Now that's more like it.'

They would now be forewarned of the Master's return.

'If only we can hold up the Master until the Doctor's got through to Tegan and Nyssa.' The Captain had another go at shutting the doors.

'Skipper!' Andrew could see the Master returning to

the TARDIS with an armful of spare parts.

There was only one place to hide. Stapley and Bilton dashed through the inner door of the control room and into the corridor.

Leaving the door very slightly ajar, the two men watched the Master kneel under the console and insert the components from his own machine.

The Master stood up and reset the co-ordinates.

'He's going to take off again. We've got to get out of here!' Andrew whispered.

But the Captain had no intention of leaving. 'The Doctor's TARDIS is our only link with the twentieth century. Where it goes, we go!'

It seemed, for the moment, that the TARDIS was going nowhere. Lights flashed, the column jerked and thumped, but the Doctor's time machine refused to dematerialise.

A gleeful Captain Stapley turned to his First Officer. 'Engine trouble?'

'That's a bit of luck.'

The smile faded from the Captain's face as he realised the implications of a serious malfunction. He voiced his fears to Andrew Bilton. 'If there is a fault in the TARDIS, we could be marooned in this wilderness for ever.'

The rage and frustration of the Master knew no bounds. He pulled more units from the inner control systems and hurled them to the floor, then strode out through the double doors.

Captain Stapley dashed back into the control room and knelt under the console. He began to remove various chipboards.

'What are you doing?' asked Andrew.

'A trouble shared is a trouble doubled,' said the Captain, replacing the modules in a random order.

'Sabotage!' Andrew grinned.

'I only hope the Doctor knows how to put all this back.'

It was a mystery to the First Officer how the Doctor could begin to cope with the baffling technology that made such a machine work. He ran his eye over the intimidating control panels. 'I thought, after Concorde, you could fly anything. But I can't make head nor tail of this …'

He would have done better, however, to have kept a watchful eye on the screen.

'I'm sorry the Doctor is not here to explain it all to you.'

Bilton and Stapley sprang guiltily to their feet. The Master had returned. He waved them away from the console with the Tissue Compression Eliminator.

'You seem to be having trouble with the TARDIS yourself,' bluffed Captain Stapley.

The Master had now quite overcome his feelings of exasperation. 'It is no longer important to me,' he replied with nonchalant charm, as he detached several more components. 'I now have all that I require. The TARDIS, for what it's worth, is yours.' Pausing only to realign the co-ordinates, he turned to the entrance and swept out.

To the dismay of Stapley and Bilton, no sooner had the Master passed through the double doors than they closed fast. Almost instantly a new sound came from the central mechanism. The column began to rise and fall; not falteringly as during the Master's attempted take-off, but with a regular rhythm. They watched, almost mesmerised by the weird motion.

After a few minutes the column slowed and stopped. Bilton and Stapley looked at each other. Where, or when had they gone?

'Look!'

Bilton followed Stapley's gaze to the screen.

They had a perfect bird's eye view of the Citadel.

'If that's a view from this ship,' said Captain Stapley, 'then the TARDIS has turned into a helicopter.'

'Easy does it,' cried Angela in a voice more used to giving instructions about seat belts.

Another stone was lifted out and the hole was big enough to climb through to the Sanctum.

The Doctor peered into the rough entrance. An unearthly light shone on his face. He was nervous now. 'You don't have to come if you don't want to,' he said, looking at the Professor.

'I'll learn nothing waiting for you here.'

The Doctor was more than grateful. 'Good man.' He turned to the passengers. 'The rest of you stay put.'

The Professor and the Doctor hauled themselves up and disappeared through the opening.

The Doctor looked round the Sanctum. He was immediately aware of the sarcophagus in the centre, but went straight to where Tegan and Nyssa lay on the ground. He knelt beside them.

To his immense relief, Tegan began to stir. She groaned and opened her eyes. 'Doctor?'

The Doctor smiled.

'I've got such a headache.' She was stunned and disorientated and could remember nothing but a great explosion.

85

'Rest a while,' said the Doctor gently.

'They willed us to come here.' Nyssa was sitting up, fully recovered, her mind still mysteriously in tune with the alien intelligence.

'Who are *they*?' asked Professor Hayter. He had hardly moved since climbing down from the hole, so humbled and awed was he by the seraphic calm of the Sanctum.

'Look in the sarcophagus, Professor,' said the Doctor.

Both men walked slowly towards the marble casket in the centre of the chamber. They peered fearfully over the edge.

A thin stratum of vapour floated above the open repository. Below the mist a great cerebellum glowed and trembled.

'It's alive!' gasped the Professor.

They stood for a moment listening to the ethereal murmer, and watching the fibrilation of the huge viscera.

Professor Hayter had never seen a living organism like it before. 'What is it?' he whispered.

'An immeasurable intelligence,' whispered the Doctor, 'at the centre of a psychic vortex. All-seeing, all-knowing.'

Tegan and Nyssa gathered round. They all stood silently, just a little afraid.

'Why did it want me to destroy it?' asked Nyssa.

The Doctor thought for a moment. 'It didn't,' he replied. 'That's why it deflected your attack.'

He explained what must have happened at the moment of explosion. A massive burst of psychokinetic energy held back the rock thrown into the sarcophagus by Nyssa, hurled the two girls to the ground, and

86

caused the beast summoned by Kalid to evaporate. So great was the power diverted to defend itself against Nyssa's physical assault, that every other manifestation of its energy was relinquished – even down to the plasmic body of Kalid. Now the force was expended.

'But why work against itself?' asked the Professor.

'Two aspects of the same personality?' suggested Nyssa.

'Jekyll and Hyde,' the Doctor nodded. 'The good and the bad.'

'The Professor was enthralled at such a perfect example of the co-existence of the Ego and the Id.

Tegan's interest was more pragmatic. 'Why should half the creature want to attack us anyway?'

The Doctor told her the worst. 'Its power is being used by the Master.'

Tegan and Nyssa were horrified to learn that the Doctor's supreme enemy was up to his old tricks, and exploiting the strange energy. But at least one part of the mighty intelligence in the sarcophagus had offered itself as their champion.

Nyssa tried to describe the force that drew them into the Sanctum and ultimately destroyed Kalid's monster, but no words of hers could convey that feeling of irresistible gravitation.

'How did you get in?' asked Hayter.

'The wall just opened.'

'Part of the benign intelligence must have triggered a hidden mechanism.'

'Did the same thing happen for you?'

The Doctor explained how they had broken down part of the wall.

'Where?' asked Tegan, surprised.

Hayter ran across to where they had made their entrance. 'The blocks have been put back!' He ran his hands over the smooth stones. All evidence of their entry had been removed.

They were trapped.

At that moment the Doctor knew – as surely as Nyssa *felt* – that the power was returning. The passengers outside would not, of their own free will, have reneged on the Doctor. They must be acting under hallucination again. Once more the invisible power haunted the Citadel. That part of the intelligence in the casket which sympathised with the Master's evil schemes was working against the Doctor and his friends, and had walled them up, helpless, inside the Sanctum.

Professor Hayter was the least anxious of the prisoners. With the passionate curiosity of an archaeologist exploring a Pharaoh's tomb, he examined the various artefacts in the chamber.

'Doctor, come and look at this.' The Professor held up a small doll-like object. 'Some sort of figurine.' He looked around him. 'There's another, and another … Could they be votive offerings? In which case, this chamber might have some religious significance.'

'Let me see that.' The Doctor took one of the figures from Professor Hayter and held it gently in his hands.

The detail was perfect. It might have been a statuette of some Greek god, only the unnatural completeness of all its features could never have been achieved by any sculptor.

'The Xeraphin,' said the Doctor in a hushed voice.

'Who are the Xeraphin?' asked Nyssa.

'They were supposed to have lived on the planet

Xerophas before it was devastated by crossfire in the Vardon–Kosnax war.'

Hayter gave a little cry. 'Please, Doctor. On top of everything else, not little green men from outer space.' But by now he was prepared to believe almost everything.

'There's nothing green about the Xeraphin,' the Doctor continued. 'The most highly developed creatures in the universe. Beings of immense mental power.'

As he examined the figurine he recognised the handywork of the Master. 'The Tissue Compression Eliminator,' he muttered.

'What's that, Doctor?'

'That little toy of the Master's. If he used it on you, your whole body would be compressed ... just like this.' And he held up the petrified homunculus.

The Professor could not understand how the Xeraphin came to be at large in the Citadel.

'They came from the sarcophagus,' explained the Doctor.

'But the thing in there is still alive, and there's only one organism,' protested Hayter.

The Doctor, however, was at last beginning to understand the nature of the intelligence in the casket, and the energy in the Citadel.

'No wonder the animus is so strong,' he gasped. 'Apart from the Master's victims, the whole race of the Xeraphin is in that sarcophagus!'

During his flying career, Flight Engineer Scobie had frequently wanted to tell his superiors to get lost. When however, he saw the Skipper and First Officer transported to oblivion before his very eyes he was appalled.

The plan had gone badly wrong. From his hiding place, Roger watched the Master scurry to and from the TARDIS, clutching various peculiar appliances. He had observed the man's temper become more and more frayed. He had finally watched him abandon the Doctor's police box, and laugh demonically as it vanished into thin air.

The idea had been for Captain Stapley and Andrew Bilton to travel with the Master and keep in touch with the TARDIS. Heaven only knew where they were now. Meanwhile the Master seemed quite happy without the Doctor's amazing machine. He collected a few more items and left the chamber.

Scobie had absolutely no idea what to do next. There was no way he could help Stapely or Bilton, so he decided to find the Doctor and explain that the Master was at large in the Citadel, and that the TARDIS had disappeared.

He crept down the corridor keeping a wary eye open for the Master.

A familiar figure in airline uniform emerged from the shadows at the far end of the corridor.

'Angela!'

'Roger!'

'Where are the others?'

She didn't answer his question. 'I can't hold out much longer.' The girl was in a bad way.

Roger Scobie realised that the hallucinations had returned, and that Angela was fighting the dream world. 'Angela, don't give up now!' He tried to comfort her and encourage her resistance. 'You mustn't let go of your mind.'

But it was obvious the poor girl was having an enormous problem resisting the illusions. How lucky for the flight deck crew that the Doctor made them reject the induction effect at the outset.

Angela was amazed that Roger could hold back the world of unreality with so little effort.

Roger Scobie explained. 'The Doctor destroyed the illusion as soon as we landed. Even when the Plasmatons got hold of us ...'

'The Doctor!' she interjected. As if he had touched a raw nerve.

'Was the Doctor with you?' Scobie needed to find him at once and explain what had happened to the TARDIS.

'The Doctor ... Yes, I think so.' She was becoming vague and sleepy again.

'Did you break through the wall? Did the Doctor get into the Sanctum?' Scobie buffeted her with questions.

'Yes.'

'Come on!'

They both hurried off down the corridor.

The hall was empty when they arrived. Roger guided Angela, as if she were a sleepwalking child, to the central rotunda.

'Angela, where did you break through?'

The girl struggled to remain conscious. 'Somewhere along here,' she answered dozily.

They continued along the line of smooth, morticed stone.

'This can't be it,' exclaimed Roger.

Angela caught her breath at the sudden stab of lucid memory. 'The power returned ... The wall was sealed!'

she blurted out.

'What!'

'I tried to stop them.' The recall of it distressed her.

'Come on!' cried Scobie. 'We've got to get him out.' He clawed at the unyielding blocks. 'The Doctor's our only link with the real world.'

'Roger!' Angela felt a sudden swell of hallucinogenic power. She was going under.

Roger did not hear her desperate appeal. 'It's no good. We'll have to go and find some tools ...' He turned from the wall. 'Angela?'

The young stewardess was walking, like a zombie, towards an incongruous Greek pillar at the far end of the hall. Roger tried to catch up with her. But he was hardly half-way before the Master appeared from behind the pillar.

Roger hugged the side of the rotunda. He could just see Angela reach the column and stand beside the Master. He heard the Master's cold commanding voice.

'Go to my TARDIS. I am the Master. You will obey me.'

Without a word the stewardess dutifully proceeded into the body of the pillar itself.

Scobie had no time to speculate on how Angela could walk into solid marble, since the Master was coming towards him. He sidled further around the rotunda.

The Master was placing his weird pieces of apparatus at regular intervals around the wall.

Roger wished there was some way of getting in touch with the Doctor. It looked as if the Master had enclosed the Sanctum in a magic circle. And if the Master's magic was as spectacular as Kalid's, then anything could happen.

The Doctor stared at the throbbing entrail in the sarcophagus. He was overwhelmed at the enormity of what the Xeraphin had achieved. 'The whole race physically amalgamated into one organism, with one massive personality,' he declared.

At the same time another piece of the jigsaw fell into place. 'That was what the Master wanted at the centre of his TARDIS.'

'Why?' asked Nyssa.

'He must have exhausted his own dynormorphic generator.'

'Of course, the nucleus is the perfect substitute.'

'And infinitely more powerful.' The Doctor shuddered. The concentrated energy of the Xeraphin harnessed to the evil will of his old enemy was an apocalyptic prospect.

Nyssa shivered. 'The power is returning.'

They all looked at the sarcophagus.

'Can't you feel it?' she moaned.

They all sensed cold like the unnatural chill of a summer eclipse. A ghostly breathing filled the chamber. The power that had already restored the phantasms outside the Sanctum was now reconsolidating its presence at the centre of the vortex.

The Doctor looked round desperately. 'We must find a way out of here!'

'Don't be afraid, Doctor. The Xeraphin is calling us.' Nyssa spoke with the icy calm of total certainty. She approached the sarcophagus.

'No, Nyssa, you'll be absorbed!' the Doctor yelled.

She was breathing heavily. 'The Xeraphin is very close.'

'Nyssa! No!'

Her eyes shone with insane joy. 'The Xeraphin contains the wisdom of the universe.' She uttered like a prophetess.

'Nyssa! Stop!'

'Without the knowledge of the Xeraphin you cannot escape from the Sanctum.' She moved closer to the casket.

'Nyssa, the knowledge will consume you!'

'The sacrifice is required; for your survival, Doctor, and the future of the Xeraphin race.'

Nyssa knelt before the sarcophagus.

An unseen hand restrained Tegan and the Doctor as they struggled to hold her back.

Nyssa offered herself to the Xeraphin.

'Stop!' The Professor stepped forward. 'I shall talk to the Xeraphin.'

'No Professor!' warned the Doctor.

But Professor Hayter was adamant. In the space of a few hours his whole life's work had been destroyed, and all that he believed in turned to nonsense. Now he was impatient to discard his own myopic view of the cosmos, and absorb the infinite knowledge of the alien race in the casket. 'I am a scientist,' he declared. 'The chance of inheriting the wisdom of the universe is an opportunity I cannot ignore.'

'It will destroy you. You don't know what you're doing.'

'Precisely, Doctor. But soon I shall know *everything*!'

'The Xeraphin welcomes you, Professor.' Nyssa

turned from the steps of the sarcophagus.

Professor Hayter moved reverently forward, sank to his knees at the edge of the casket, and waited for the moment of apotheosis.

For a few seconds there was calm in the Sanctum. Then came the gusting of a great wind. The Professor trembled as if gripped by some profound emotion. He sobbed. He convulsed. He groaned. He began to writhe in alternate paroxysms of agony and ecstasy. His whole body palpitated. He gave a cry of utter perturbation.

He was dead.

The Doctor first checked that Nyssa was all right. Apart from her distress at the violent demise of Professor Hayter, she seemed her normal self. As the Professor reached out to the mind of the Xeraphin, her own link with the intelligence had been broken.

They all stood round Hayter's body, subdued and depressed. The Professor's fatal contact with the Xeraphin had done nothing to help them escape from the Sanctum.

'If only we could find the door,' said Tegan. Together with the Doctor she walked around the circular wall examining every stone.

Nyssa never took her eyes off the lifeless Professor. 'Look!' she suddenly cried.

Tegan and the Doctor stared at the dead man. The Professor's body seethed as if consumed by a million invisible locusts.

'The whole molecular structure is breaking apart,' exclaimed the Doctor.

Soon, all that had been Hayter, his clothes, and his shoes were reduced to a shimmering cloud of minute particles which rose up and floated over the sarcophagus. A beam of light shone upward from the casket irradiating the hovering nimbus and drawing it out into a thin plume.

A spectral image began to form in the cloud like a photographic impression.

'I think the Xeraphin is trying to materialise,' whispered the Doctor.

Unearthly features started to reveal themselves, matching the detail of the compressed figures the Professor had discovered, but now projected lifesize.

A transfigured Xeraphin stood before them. The apparition spoke.

'I am Anithon of the race of the Xeraphin.'

They felt dwarfed by the presence of such an unworldly creature.

'I come in this shape as ambassador of our people.' Anithon spoke again.

'What are the Xeraphin doing on Earth?' the Doctor addressed the ghostly envoy.

'Our homeland was laid waste by barbarians, so we travelled to this deserted planet to build a new home for our people.'

'That explains the spaceship we saw,' thought Tegan.

'But the sickness followed us,' sighed Anithon.

'Radiation poisoning,' said the Doctor. And Nyssa remembered the sickening vision of death and disease that came to her as she stepped off Concorde.

The Xeraphin continued: 'Using our psychic power we melded into a unity.'

'You achieved the absorption of a whole race into a single bioplasmic body?'

'Yes, Doctor. In that shape we planned to rest until the contamination was passed. Then we could regenerate.'

'What went wrong?'

The face of Anithon darkened with despair. 'At the moment of regeneration the Time Lord came, seeking our power.'

'The Master!' The Doctor had suspected as much.

'Those who were first reborn were destroyed.'

The Doctor looked down for a moment at the victims of the Master's vile weapon.

'We were forced to retreat to our resting place.'

There was still one thing that puzzled the Doctor. He turned again to Anithon. 'How did the Master gain so much control of your psychic power?'

'Through the projection of his mind he communicated with our baseness.'

'But surely there is more good than evil in the Xeraphin.'

Anithon groaned. A shadow passed across his face. 'The schismatic effect of the Time Lord's intervention ... We are infinitely divided!' He gave a cry of pain. 'Listen carefully.' He spoke quickly, with the desperation of a dying man's confession. 'Together we can secure the safety of yourself and your friends and the regeneration of our race.'

'We'll have to deal with the Master first.'

'That is possible. I will explain ...' An agonising groan issued from the creature. A dark cancer was swelling within him. From Anithon erupted a second Xeraphin.

'I am Zarak, of the race of the Xeraphin.'

The Master knew that time was running out. If the Doctor could communicate with the white Xeraphin all his plans would come to nothing; he would never control the Xeraphin energy, and he would be marooned for ever in the frozen wilderness. He frantically inserted the remaining components into the cable around the rotunda.

'My brother has misled you.' A glowering Zarak addressed the Doctor. 'We need no help. The Xeraphin has a new destiny.'

'No, Zarak,' Anithon cried desperately. 'The ambition of the Master will destroy our race.'

'For the new to be born, the old must die,' chimed Zarak mechanically.

'No Zarak!'

'We are the new power. The force that binds and shapes.'

The Doctor's blood ran cold. How completely the Master had subverted the selfish, acquisitive members of the Xeraphin race to his purpose! Zarak even sounded like the Master.

The braggart voice continued. 'We shall be feared and adored. Nations will prostrate themselves before us. We shall be Divinity.'

'Zarak, that's just a dream.' The Doctor appealed to common sense. 'The Master will use your power for his own evil purposes. The Xeraphin race will never be able to regenerate.'

Anithon, encouraged by the Doctor, turned to his other half. 'Zarak,' he appealed. 'Do you not yearn for shape and touch and feeling!' He spoke with the frustrated longing of centuries. 'My brother, our true destiny is the becoming of ourselves.'

Zarak scowled. But he was suddenly less sure of himself.

Anithon pressed home the attack. 'All our power

must be combined to work with the Doctor against the rebel Time Lord.'

Nyssa turned and whispered to the Doctor. 'I think we're winning.'

'Winning what, for heaven's sake?' Tegan had no idea what was going on.

In a hushed voice the Doctor explained the fateful debate between the good and the evil Xeraphin, represented by Anithon and Zarak.

'Whatever side wins the argument will control the combined power.'

Zarak was losing ground. 'You talk me out of my purpose, brother Anithon,' he snarled. 'But other counsels will prevail.'

'It is forbidden!' shouted Anithon.

'In the new order nothing is forbidden,' cried a defiant Zarak.

'No!' Anithon was aghast at such heresy.

Zarak began to call in an impassioned voice. 'Come forth, Kalistoran! Come forth, Alkarim! Come forth, Vaan!'

The chamber grew dark.

'What's happening now?' whispered Tegan.

'Zarak is summoning more evil Xeraphin,' cried the Doctor.

'Come to me, Zarindas! Come to me, Mordaal!' Zarak continued the terrible muster.

'Help me, Doctor!' begged Anithon.

The Doctor had never felt more impotent. 'How can we help you!'

'With our minds!' shouted Nyssa. 'We must will the dark Xeraphin not to appear.'

They instinctively joined hands and concentrated on

holding back the rising tide of evil.

The Master knew that the moment of supreme crisis had come. He completed his adjustments to the loop and rushed to his TARDIS.

Sweat poured from the faces of the Doctor, Tegan and Nyssa.

'I can't keep this up much longer,' moaned Tegan.

'You must,' gasped the Doctor.

Zarak quivered as the shadowy figures of unborn Xeraphin tried to thrust themselves from him. But the will of the Doctor and Nyssa and Tegan restrained his evil confrères.

'I think we've done it!' cried Nyssa.

'Zarak!' It was Anithon who spoke. 'Embrace again the ancient truth of the Xeraphin.'

But Zarak gave a sudden bellow of triumph. 'Too late my brother! The Master is ready for us.'

There was a grinding sound and the entire sarcophagus dematerialised. For a moment the wraith-like shapes of Anithon and Zarak hung in the air, then, no longer supported, drifted to the ground in a flurry of dust.

'The Master has perfected the induction loop,' said the Doctor in a shocked voice.

'But what's happened to the Xeraphin?' asked Tegan.

'Transferred to the centre of the Master's TARDIS.' Nyssa was as appalled as the Doctor.

Tegan still did not understand. The Doctor turned to explain. She had never seen that ashen look on his face before. He was abject with despair.

'It means that the Master has finally defeated me,' said the Doctor.

9

On a Wing and a Prayer

It was particularly galling for two pilots to be in a flying machine and totally unable to effect a landing.

'We must be in a perpetual holding pattern.' Andrew Bilton was looking at the TARDIS screen and its unchanging view of the Citadel some two thousand feet below.

The Captain had been scrutinising every switch and lever on the console. Nothing related to any kind of flying control that he had ever encountered. But he had no intention of staying indefinitely in this hovering prison. If they didn't help themselves, it was unlikely anyone else would. 'I'm going to have a go at flying this thing,' he announced.

'Are you sure?' A couple of lines of an old song ran through Andrew's mind; something about scraping strawberry jam from the tarmac ...

'What other choice have we got?' the Captain demanded.

He chose a small lever at the side of the console. At least it looked like a throttle. Perhaps, if he could induce some slight lateral movement, he would get enough confidence to try a vertical manoeuvre. He eased the slider forward. For a moment nothing happened. Then, to the accompaniment of a most disturbing whine, the TARDIS lurched violently to one side.

Bilton and Stapley were thrown across the control room. As the Captain struggled to reach the console, the whole room tilted in the opposite direction. Stapley caught hold of the central panel as he shot past. A steady and sickening roll now developed as the TARDIS see-sawed from one side to the other. Captain Stapley hauled himself up from the floor and returned the lever to its original setting.

Slowly the TARDIS settled on an even keel.

'Not a good idea,' observed Captain Stapley, who had not experienced such a rough ride since a mechanical descent by a young First Officer on the simulator at Filton. 'I don't think we'll risk touching the controls.'

Bilton couldn't agree more.

'If there was a radio ...' The Captain was still determined to escape. 'We might be able to send a Mayday signal.'

'Who's going to answer it?' His co-pilot was less optimistic.

'Perhaps the Doctor has a remote navigational ...' He got no further.

'What's the matter, Skipper?'

Captain Stapley was staring in utter disbelief over Andrew Bilton's shoulder, at the entrance to the inner TARDIS. 'How did you get in here?'

In the doorway stood Professor Hayter. Without saying a word, the Professor moved slowly towards them.

The Doctor sat on the floor of the empty Sanctum. He was profoundly depressed. He took no interest in the efforts of Tegan and Nyssa to find where the stones had been loosened.

'If the Master's installed the Xeraphin in his TARDIS, there's no limit to his powers,' he said dejectedly. He realised that they had been fighting not only the Master, but half the Xeraphin race – possibly the most brilliant minds in the universe. Kalid had been a disguise, not only for his old adversary, but a focus for the minds of the evil Xeraphin.

'There must be some way to stop the Master.' Tegan had more fight in her.

The Doctor suddenly felt ashamed that he had been willing to give up so easily. He looked round the Sanctum, but with the Xeraphin gone, there was no way of releasing the doors and finding the way back through the cunning labyrinth that had delivered Tegan and Nyssa to the inner chamber.

He got to his feet and walked over to the collection of rocks from which Nyssa had launched her bombardment of the nucleus. They were indeed amazingly heavy – doubtless souvenirs from the home planet.

With a rock apiece they all three battered the wall of the Sanctum. But for all their weight, the strange mineral lumps disintegrated on contact with the stone of the chamber. They would need help from outside. But the Doctor could think of no way of making contact. He fought back another wave of despair.

'Listen!' The girls' sharp ears had picked up a familiar sound.

In the space left by the sarcophagus they could see the nascent shape of the TARDIS. The Doctor was flabbergasted. Only the Master would have been able to navigate his time machine. But with the Xeraphin on board his own vehicle, he should have no further interest in the Sanctum or any use for the Doctor's TARDIS.

They all hid behind the police box as the door opened. The Doctor crept to the corner and peered round. The sight of Captain Stapley and Andrew Bilton standing in the entrance delighted him. He rushed forward and grasped Stapley by the hand.

'Are we glad to see you, Doctor!' said the Captain.

'Are we glad to see the TARDIS!' said Tegan.

'My dear Captain, you really are the most remarkable man.' The Doctor was beaming. 'To pilot the TARDIS, and with such precision.'

The Doctor, thought the Captain, has rather got the wrong end of the stick; but before he could explain they were all shepherded through the door of the TARDIS.

'You have control, as they say.' The Doctor waved Captain Stapley towards the console, still astounded at the Concorde pilot's uncanny knack with co-ordinates.

The Captain was quick to explain that, in any travelling by phone box, he and Bilton were strictly passengers.

'Then how did you pilot yourself here?' asked Nyssa.

'The Professor, of course,' answered Andrew.

'What!'

'Didn't you instruct him on how to fly the TARDIS?'

'No,' said the Doctor quietly.

Bilton looked round the console room. 'Where is the Professor? He was here a moment ago.'

There was an eery silence. Saying nothing, the Doctor began to set the co-ordinates. It was left to Tegan to break the news to Bilton and Stapley. She spoke quietly and unemotionally. 'Professor Hayter is dead.'

Scobie wanted desperately to help the passengers. They stood in a long crocodile beside the rotunda, like a queue at a check-in desk. In fact, several had visas and boarding cards in their hands. He made a quick count of the uniforms amongst the crowd; nine of them. Except for Professor Hayter this must be the full complement of flight 192. If only he could keep them all together.

But the Master, the Tissue Compression Eliminator in his hand, prowled like a wolf round a flock of sheep. Scobie stayed in the shadows.

The line moved forward. First one, then another, then another of the waiting men and women walked straight into the pillar. Roger Scobie was no longer even surprised. Anything could happen in this place.

And it did. With a whirring and a clattering, the column, the passengers, the crew members and the Master all vanished.

No-one on board the Doctor's TARDIS could explain how Professor Hayter could have appeared in the control room and set the co-ordinates so accurately for the Sanctum.

'A telepathic projection?' hazarded the Doctor.

'Perhaps he isn't dead,' suggested Nyssa.

'The man was atomised!' Tegan had seen it with her own eyes.

'No!' Nyssa spoke again with that sudden mysterious insight. 'He was absorbed into the Xeraphin life force.'

The Doctor now knew that all was not lost. Even the

Xeraphin – at least the *white* Xeraphin – were fighting back.

For a while after the departure of the Master, Roger Scobie was alone in the great hall. He thought, for a rather sobering minute or two, that he might be alone in the whole Citadel, perhaps the only example of *Homo sapiens* in the entire prehistoric world. It was a great comfort to see the Doctor's TARDIS materialise in front of him.

'Roger, you're safe!' The Captain ran towards his Flight Engineer.

'This place is getting just like Heathrow,' joked Scobie, disguising, with a quick wisecrack, the extent of his relief.

The Doctor overheard him. 'Have you seen another TARDIS?'

'Would that be a sort of Greek pillar?'

'Could well be.'

'It disappeared a few minutes ago.'

'We've lost him!' exclaimed Nyssa in dismay.

The Doctor didn't think so. 'The Master must still be in the same time zone, and probably not far away.'

'How do you know that?'

The Master's TARDIS won't be fully operational yet. He's got the nucleus inside all right, but he'll need to work on it.'

Scobie was explaining to Bilton and Stapley what had happened to Captain Urquhart and his passengers. 'Like animals into the ark. I've heard of a football team getting into a telephone kiosk, but this was ridiculous ...' He stopped. The Doctor was staring at him, a look of horror on his face.

'Come on!' Before anyone had a chance to explain relative dimension to a mystified engineer, the Doctor had disappeared back into the TARDIS.

They all trooped in after him.

The Doctor feverishly punched in new co-ordinates. 'Captain Stapley, the passengers are now in greater danger than ever before.' Without further explanation he turned to Nyssa. 'Take the TARDIS back to the Concorde cargo hold. Tegan, you come with me.' Half-way to the doors he turned back to Captain Stapley. 'Captain, I want you to get your plane ready for take-off immediately.'

Captain Stapley reeled at the staggering optimism of the man. It was all very well leap-frogging about in an old police box, but Concorde was something else. Had the man no idea how the aircraft gobbled up tarmac before getting airborne? The facilities needed for start-up? The damage done by that crash landing?

The Doctor smiled hopefully. 'Wing and a prayer, Captain?' His enthusiasm was contagious.

'I suppose we could cannibalise Victor Foxtrot for spare parts,' suggested Roger Scobie.

'That mudflat could never be rougher than the runway at Kennedy,' conceded Andrew Bilton.

And even Captain Stapley had the idea for a cunning lash-up to start the jets.

'The co-ordinates are all set,' shouted the Doctor to Nyssa and hurried off with Tegan.

The Tardis reappeared on its side in the hold of the Concorde. The Captain was first out, hauling himself through the door of the police box. He quickly briefed his co-pilot and engineer. 'Andrew, you and I will start the cockpit checks. Roger, I want you to do a preliminary walk-round of the aircraft.'

Nyssa wandered round the stalk-like legs of the aircraft with Roger Scobie. It was an alien, mechanistic technology to the noble woman from Traken. She gazed up at the delta shape above her like a tourist at a mediaeval cathedral.

Roger pored over the undercarriage mechanism. 'The brakeline's fractured and we've lost a lot of fluid,' he pronounced.

'Is that bad?' Nyssa asked innocently.

'Bad?' The engineer grinned. 'It's a miracle! We can probably nick the spares from Victor Foxtrot.' Scobie picked up his tools and started to walk the couple of hundred yards to the other Concorde. He stopped. 'Do you see that?'

The distant aircraft shimmered like a calm sea at sunrise. Then the moment passed. They decided it was a bit of mist or a trick of the light and moved on.

The footsteps of Tegan and the Doctor echoed through the deserted Citadel. At every bend, every doorway, every dark corner, the Doctor looked round nervously. 'Keep your eyes open,' he whispered to Tegan. 'The Master could be anywhere.'

'Why did the Master take the passengers?' asked Tegan as they walked.

'Molecular disintegration,' answered the Doctor. 'That way he's got a neat little store of protoplasm with which he can do anything he wants.'

'Melt them down?' Tegan felt sick. 'We've got to stop him!' she cried.

When they reached Kalid's chamber, it was obvious the bird had flown. The pedestal beneath the crystal had been ransacked for its components. Nor was there any sign of the modules the Master had removed from the Doctor's TARDIS. But the Doctor knew the Master could not have gone far. His TARDIS must be somewhere near the Citadel – in a new disguise perhaps.

A terrible thought came to him. 'Quickly!' he shouted to Tegan. 'We've got to get back to Captain Stapley!'

The Doctor and Tegan left the Citadel behind them and strode across the hard frozen earth. Tegan imagined how the centuries would erode that great monolithic pyramid, till, in her own day, there was no evidence it ever existed. As she scanned the primordial landscape, she tried to visualise the motorway, the airport hotels, the housing estates to which they were so anxious to return.

The Doctor's thoughts were less philosophical. He stopped as he spotted the two Concordes on the horizon. 'Just as I thought!' he cried. 'Come on!'

'What's the damage, Roger?' Captain Stapley swung round from his instrument check as Scobie poked his head into the narrow cockpit.

'Fractured brakeline.'

'Is that all?' Bilton couldn't believe their luck. 'Not a bad landing, Skipper!'

'Can you repair it?'

'With a bit of luck, and a bit of Victor Foxtrot.'

They were delighted at the sheer resilience of the aircraft. Only one problem remained. They had no way of starting the engines.

Captain Stapley smiled rather smugly. He had an ingenious scheme for providing the vital compressed air. 'We'll take the tyres off one and four wheels of Victor Foxtrot.'

Roger chuckled. It was a damn good idea. But there was one little snag ... 'Skipper, have you any idea how we jack up a hundred tons of aircraft?'

'We dig a hole,' said Captain Stapley.

You've got to hand it to him, thought Andrew Bilton, impressed with the Captain's lateral thinking.

'With three and two wheels still in place you don't need to support her,' cried Scobie.

The Doctor ran towards the parked aircraft, leaving Tegan far behind. He was panting heavily as he met up with Nyssa and the crew who were about to start work on the undercarriage of Victor Foxtrot. 'Captain,' he asked Stapley, 'is your aircraft all right?'

'Apart from some damage to the hydraulics, but we'll take some bits of Victor Foxtrot.'

'Ah,' said the Doctor. 'Not a good idea.' Thank goodness he had stopped them in time.

'But, Doctor, it would work.'

'If that were Concorde.'

Now the Doctor's being ridiculous, thought Stapley.

'It *is* Concorde!' protested Scobie.

Logic, however, was on the Doctor's side. He pointed to the second plane. 'That aircraft was damaged. Now it's in perfect condition.'

He was absolutely right.

'We must be hallucinating again,' groaned the Captain.

'I'm afraid not,' said the Doctor. 'That's the Master's TARDIS.'

Roger Scobie gulped. This was worse than a hundred people hitching a lift in a lump of marble. 'It's a plane!' He tried hard not to sound narrow-minded, but really!

For the Doctor and his companions the situation was horribly familiar.

'The Master has operated his chameleon circuit.'

'And materialised round the other aircraft.'

The Captain was desperately trying to follow the bizarre reasoning. 'Then Victor Foxtrot ...' he stammered.

'Is inside the Master's TARDIS,' the Doctor concluded sharply. 'I wish I had time to explain dimensional transcendentalism,' he added, already half-way to Captain Stapley's genuine Concorde. 'I'm going into my own TARDIS,' he shouted. 'You all stay here.'

'No, Doctor!' called Nyssa in alarm, trying to catch up with him. 'It's too dangerous!'

'There's no other way!'

'What are you going to do?' asked Stapley, trying to get a word in edgeways.

'The Doctor's going to materialise round the Master's TARDIS,' said Nyssa, horrified at the risk.

'You know what happened before!' Tegan had her own nightmare memories of those Chinese puzzles, from when she first stumbled into the TARDIS.

The Doctor would not be stopped. 'There's no time for anything else,' he called from the cabin door.

But there was no time for anything at all.

'We're too late,' groaned Nyssa, as the dreaded clattering reached them from across the mudflat.

111

Then there was only one Concorde left parked on the frozen tundra. The Master had gone.

'With the power of the Xeraphin, the Master will be invincible,' declared Nyssa.

And we're stuck, thought the Doctor. 'Without the bits he stole from my TARDIS, we can only travel in this time zone,' he explained to the others.

'We're marooned?' asked Tegan in disbelief.

'I'm afraid so.'

Before anyone could think of anything to say, another whirring sound filled the air. They all looked up to see the shape of Golf Victor Foxtrot rematerialise a short way from their own aircraft.

The Doctor was not a man to take pleasure in the misfortunes of others, but a broad smile lit up his face. The Master was stuck as well.

The Master flung open the door of his Concorde TARDIS and glared at the Doctor. 'Devious to the last,' he hissed.

'Technical hitch?' Butter wouldn't melt in the Doctor's mouth as he smiled innocently at his enraged enemy.

'Your substitution of the time lapse compressor, for the temporal limiter,' accused the Master.

'That's the way it goes,' the Doctor chided infuriatingly, 'if you will steal other people's property.' Leaving the Master on the point of apoplexy, he swung round to Nyssa. 'What's he talking about?' he whispered. 'Have you been tampering with my TARDIS?'

'Of course not.'

'Just imagine what would have happened if I had tried to go forward with the temporal limiter patched into the time lapse compression circuit ...'

Captain Stapley felt like a schoolboy who had got his best friend into trouble. He coughed politely. 'Doctor, I think I can explain.'

'You, Captain?' said the Doctor, very surprised if he could.

'When we were in the TARDIS, I swapped some of the parts round. Thought it might put a spanner in the works.'

The Doctor's eyes were already twinkling.

'Stupid really ...' the Captain apologised.

Grinning from ear to ear, the Doctor grasped Stapley by the hand. 'Stupid?' he shouted. 'It was brilliant!'

The Master was straining to hear what was going on below. The Doctor smiled up at him. 'Your prospects seem rather limited, Master.'

Through the Master's mind raced a thousand and one exquisite tortures he would like to inflict on the Doctor. He restrained himself from telling the Doctor all about them. Unfortunately, the ball, just for the moment, was in the Doctor's court. 'I can still operate my TARDIS,' he replied.

'Yes. But such a limited range.'

The Doctor had him there. 'Very well. What are your terms?'

'You free the passengers,' demanded the Doctor, 'we have access to both aircraft, and you return all the components of my TARDIS that are no longer necessary for the normal functioning of your machine.'

'And what will you give me?'

'The temporal limiter,' bargained the Doctor.

It was a hard decision for the Master. His old enemy

would be able to escape. But he needed the temporal limiter, and with the Xeraphin life force in his TARDIS the Doctor would not outwit him for much longer ...

The Master slammed the door.

'Has he agreed?' asked Stapley.

'We'll know in a moment.'

'Look!' shouted Andrew.

The Corinthian column had appeared a few yards away.

'There's the real Concorde,' said Tegan, pointing to the aircraft with its torn wing and dislocated engine pod.

'The Master's accepted,' cried Nyssa as Captain Urquhart's passengers began to emerge from the marble fluting.

'Captain,' said the Doctor to Stapley who was staring in disbelief at the improbable disembarkation, 'I need your aircraft ready for take-off as soon as possible.'

Stapley pulled himself together. 'Andrew, Roger ... We'll need to measure the length of that runway.' They all went across to examine the stretch of frozen mud.

'You two stay here,' the Doctor ordered Tegan and Nyssa. He walked slowly to the Master's TARDIS. The Master stood in the doorway, in his arms a pile of vital equipment. Not a word was spoken. The Doctor took the pieces one by one. The two Time Lords stared impassively at each other. 'You seem to have mislaid the quantum accelerator.' The Doctor was the first to break the silence.

'Not at all, Doctor. You shall have it when you give me the correctly programmed temporal limiter.'

Their distrust was mutual.

The Doctor turned and hurried back to where his

TARDIS was waiting in the Concorde hold.

Bilton and Scobie attacked the frozen ground around the four-wheel bogey of Victor Foxtrot's starboard undercarriage. The earth was like concrete and they were soon sweating profusely. At least they were warmer than Tegan who stood beside them shivering, waiting to help take the weight of the wheel, once the soil had been removed from under it.

'Doctor, I'll need an external power supply for the start-up, 400 cycles, 115 volts,' Captain Stapley called into the control room.

'Very well, Captain.' Nyssa prepared to run a line from the TARDIS.

'Easy now.' Tegan helped Roger and Andrew lift the second wheel clear of the support. They stood for a moment getting their breath back. Just as well the soil was so hard and icy, thought Tegan, or the remaining two wheels might have slipped into the excavation, bringing the whole aircraft down on top of them.

'Right,' said Roger Scobie, 'you and Andrew roll those wheels across to Alpha Charlie. I'm going on board Victor Foxtrot to rip out a reduction valve and some trunking from the air-conditioning, then I'll strip the components for our own undercarriage.'

Tegan and Andrew raised one of the wheels and began to trundle it towards the other Concorde. I've been here before, thought Tegan, with a sudden flash of *déjà vu*; then realised how similar were the wheels of the airliner to Aunt Vanessa's sports car.

The Doctor soon replaced the components that had been pilfered by the Master.

Nyssa watched him scramble round under the console. She was uneasy. 'Doctor, you haven't got the quantum accelerator back from the Master.'

And he hasn't got the temporal limiter,' replied the Doctor as he slid out the essential module from where it had been hidden by Captain Stapley. 'The idea is to keep him waiting until we're ready to take off.'

Nyssa was terrified at the idea of trying to get airborne again in Concorde. With the quantum accelerator in place, the TARDIS would be working as well as ever. Why couldn't they all go back in that?

'I need the TARDIS to deal with the Master,' said the Doctor.

'How?'

'I'm thinking about it,' replied the Doctor enigmatically.

Ice-cold fluid dribbled over Roger Scobie's hands and down his sleeve as he removed the damaged brakeline. The replacement was standing by; in a few moments the undercarriage would be repaired.

Beneath the port inner engine Tegan helped Andrew with a bundle of tubing which the co-pilot was connecting to the valve of one of the tyres. 'Two and three engines have to be started with an external air supply,' he explained. 'One and four then start internally.'

'Undercarriage fixed!' A grubby but cheerful Scobie slipped into the flight-deck.

'Well done, Roger.'

Nyssa's head appeared in the door behind him. 'External power all right, Captain?'

'Yes.' Captain Stapley started to get out of the left-hand seat. 'Tell the Doctor we're ready, will you, please?' Nyssa scurried back towards the cargo hold. 'Roger, I want to do a final walk-round of the aircraft

116

while we're waiting for the Doctor.' The Captain scrambled from the cockpit with his engineer.

The Master watched all the activity like a hawk. He knew the Doctor was playing for time, but he would give him so much leeway ... and no more. He strode towards Tegan.

Tegan, kneeling over the wheel, saw the black figure out of the corner of her eye. She turned; the Master loomed over her.

'I am impatient to leave this place. Tell the Doctor I require the temporal limiter immediately, or I shall start to eliminate your passengers.' He held the deadly black weapon between his fingers as casually as if it were a cigarette holder. But Tegan knew that his promise was no idle threat.

'Captain Stapley says the aircraft is ready,' announced Nyssa, returning to the TARDIS control room.

'Good,' said the Doctor as he tinkered with the temporal limiter. 'Another few minutes.'

Tegan ran in, breathless from the gymnastics involved in reaching the TARDIS. 'Doctor, hurry up!' she shouted. 'The Master's getting trigger-happy out there.'

'Then we'd better not keep him waiting.' The Doctor picked up the temporal limiter.

'Looks fine, Roger,' said the Captain as he examined the repaired undercarriage.

Roger was as pleased as punch at his make do and mend, but was apprehensive at the impending take-off.

They all looked at the mudflat stretching away to the horizon, and quietly said a prayer. 'No knowing what'll

117

happen going over that ground at two hundred knots,' muttered Scobie.

'What happens when we get airborne?' asked Bilton, looking on the bright side.

'Up to the Doctor isn't it?'

The Doctor walked the short distance to the Master's TARDIS. The Master was waiting for him.

'The temporal limiter,' demanded the Master.

'The quantum accelerator,' insisted the Doctor.

Neither trusted the other a millimetre. The Master guardedly revealed the Doctor's accelerator. The Doctor allowed a glimpse of the Master's limiter. There was a fumbling, mutual snatch and grab. The deal was done.

'Shall I say *au revoir*, Doctor?' The Master oozed venomous charm.

The Doctor turned his back dismissively on his arch enemy and returned to the plane. Hardly had the Master, with a dark chuckle, entered his TARDIS than the column dematerialised.

By now none of the crew batted an eyelid. 'I suppose he could end up anywhere in the universe,' said Captain Stapley.

'Heathrow, actually.'

The Doctor's casual announcement caused consternation.

'He's virtually running in a new TARDIS,' he went on to explain. 'To check out the temporal dimensions he'll need to track back the line of the time contour.'

Andrew Bilton was appalled at what the Doctor had just allowed to happen.

'He'll land up in London with the nucleus on board?'

118

'Yes.'

'It's a disaster!'

'Quite right.' The Doctor couldn't agree more. 'Shall we go on board?'

All around them dazed passengers were returning, once again, to their senses.

'The punters are your responsibility, Tegan,' shouted Stapley, making a quick escape to the main door. 'When you get them on board, stand by on those tyres.'

Just my luck, thought Tegan. My first job as a stewardess. She tried to forget how dirty and sweaty she was and approached the passengers with a radiant smile on her face. 'Ladies and gentlemen, we do apologise for the delay ...' The words flowed like syrup. 'Your flight to Heathrow is now ready for boarding. Would you proceed to the aircraft immediately.'

The Doctor soon had the quantum accelerator back in circuit. He stood up from the console looking very pleased with himself. Nyssa couldn't understand why. 'The Master will get to Earth before us,' she fretted.

'Not with my temporal limiter in circuit,' the Doctor reassured her.

'It won't work?'

'Of course it will. You don't think I could fool the Master do you?' He started to make his way out of the TARDIS and towards the flight deck. Nyssa recognised the glint in his eye. She smiled. 'Mind you,' said the Doctor, 'there is an inhibition factor inherent in the programming.'

'What does that mean?'

The Doctor grinned. 'We get to Heathrow first.'

Tegan felt very lonely out in the cold beside the two wheels, with everyone else strapped in their seats waiting for take-off. She looked up at the flight deck window, hoping for the sign to release the compressed air.

But with such a hazardous launch before them, the pre-flight checks were more vital than at any well-equipped international airport.

The moment came.

'Air on number three engine.' Captain Stapley gave the order in a calm, clipped voice.

Tegan released the valve. There was a hiss like a soda syphon. She prayed that not too much air was escaping from the makeshift connection.

'Start number three engine.'

From the right hand side of the airfcraft came a dull whine.

'Start number two engine.'

Another deep snarl from the left of the plane.

'Air off. Get Tegan in.'

The air jets were screaming now, and Tegan had her hands over her ears as Bilton waved to her. She pulled the feed clear and ran for the door.

'I want reverse thrust on three and four so I can turn the aircraft.'

The engines roared as the plane rotated anticlockwise.

The Captain was giving his final briefing to his First Officer and Engineer when the Doctor arrived on the flight deck. 'I will abandon take-off, prior to V1, only on the loss of two engines …'

'Ready to go?' asked the Doctor.

'Strap yourself in for take-off will you please,

Doctor,' ordered Captain Stapley. He turned back to Bilton and Scobie. 'At V2 we will maintain our climb-out at theta two under full power.'

Captain Stapley looked ahead at the frozen mudflat. No one at Toulouse or Bristol ever dreamed she would have to come unstuck from that. He glanced over his shoulder at the Doctor. 'Cross your fingers.' He beamed the merest smile in the direction of Bilton and Scobie. 'This is it, gentlemen.'

The Captain's right hand rested on the four throttles. 'Three, two, one ...' He counted the seconds. 'Now.' He pushed the throttles hard against the end stop.

The idling turbines surged to a full-throated roar. The great silver creature struggled forward.

There were rolling. Faster, faster. A bit of feedback already shaking the stick.

'Airspeed building.'

Four green lights on the instrument panel; after-burners coming in. Flame from the four Olympus engines; full power.

Faster, faster.

'One hundred knots.'

'Power checked,' called Scobie.

'V1,' called Bilton.

One hundred and seventy knots and building, Alpha Charlie rocketed down the mudflat. No stopping now; it was take-off or crash.

The passengers in the cabin had never known such a buffeting. Captain Stapley, hands on the shaking control column, felt every bump from the primitive runway. Bilton, eyes on the airspeed indicator, willed the needle to the next marker.

Five hundred yards of runway left. A rocky hillside

rushing closer. One eight seven, one eight eight, one eight nine, one ninety knots ...

'Rotate,' called Bilton, and Captain Stapley eased the column towards him.

Concorde Golf Alpha Charlie lifted her nose skyward, careered a little further on her main wheels, and was airborne. Four vapour trails streaming behind, she soared above the Citadel.

Captain Stapley was as excited as a child. 'What did I tell you, Doctor,' he shouted jubilantly. 'Finest plane in the world!'

The Doctor just managed a smile. There was a moment as they thundered towards the rocks that he wished they had gone by TARDIS.

'Gear up,' called the Captain. Andrew and Roger, who had shared the Doctor's feelings, grinned sheepishly at each other and set about the routine business of maintaining the climb. 'Where to now, Doctor?' asked Stapley.

The Doctor extricated himself from the jump seat, leaned between the two pilots and started to programme the flight computer.

10

In Transit

Tegan and Nyssa wondered how the Doctor was going to get them all back to the twentieth century. They had certainly never seen him enter such elaborate co-ordinates. He stood up and thought for a moment, checked, double-checked, and corrected a setting.

'Now.' The Doctor looked at the girls. 'As we dematerialise, we reverse the process of the time contour and kick Concorde back on its original flight path ...' He sounded very confident. But as he activated the controls, Tegan couldn't help noticing he had his fingers crossed.

The dematerialisation of the TARDIS had an immediate effect on the flight deck.

'Centre of gravity's shifted,' called Roger as he instinctively corrected the trim of the aircraft.

But the alteration in payload was not the only change. 'The radio navigation's working!' shouted Andrew delightedly.

Captain Stapley scanned the dials. One by one all the instruments were coming back to life.

The radio crackled. 'Golf Alpha Charlie, permission to descend to three five zero.' His voice betrayed none of the emotion he felt. They might have been for a joyride round the Bay of Biscay. But there was a roguish smile on his face as he turned to Roger and

Andrew. 'We're back!' he said.

Meanwhile the TARDIS had taken good care of the Doctor, Tegan and Nyssa. The door opened and they peeped out at the hurly-burly of Heathrow. It was hard to believe, with the screaming chorus of jets and the reek of aviation fuel, that this was the same location as the Citadel.

'We appear to be on time for a change,' observed the Doctor optimistically, though the significance of this escaped the two girls.

Nyssa watched in amazement as a jumbo lifted into the sky with an ear-splitting screech. 'What a funny way to travel,' she shouted above the din.

'Kind of fun, though,' said Tegan, feeling a pang of nostalgia that quite surprised her.

Nyssa had never seen that faraway look on Tegan's face before. 'You miss it, don't you?'

'Oh, I don't know.' It was a while before Tegan turned from watching the activity on the runway. 'It's not exactly dull with the Doctor.'

Their sentimental tête-à-tête was not to continue. Two policemen were hurrying towards the TARDIS.

'Doctor!' called Nyssa in dismay.

To the girls' surprise, the Doctor looked up in the air. 'What we need,' he said, studiously ignoring the approach of the Law, 'is a diversion. And with a bit of luck, not to mention judgement ...'

Tegan wondered why the two constables had stopped. They too were looking upwards.

'Look!' shouted Nyssa.

In the sky, above the TARDIS, shining brighter than Haley's Comet, was a Corinthian column.

'The Master's TARDIS,' cried Tegan. She looked at the Doctor, but he was already running into his own TARDIS.

'The Master can't land,' cried Nyssa as she watched the Doctor frantically punching in new co-ordinates.

'No. Same co-ordinates as the TARDIS. But we got here first ...' He gave a deep sigh. 'Just!'

The two constables had been surprised to discover a police box outside the Terminal building. The subsequent appearance in the sky of a pillar of fire caused the younger man to wonder if the Day of Judgement was at hand. His older colleague suspected a few too many at lunch-time. Neither of them was reassured by the disappearance of the illicit box. But at least the shining column had vanished as well.

'It's gone,' said Nyssa, watching the TARDIS screen.

'Knocked back into time-space like a straight six into the pavilion,' declared the Doctor with great satisfaction.

Nyssa's face suffused with sadness. 'The Xeraphin will never be able to regenerate.'

The Doctor smiled. 'They stand a much better chance on their own planet,' he said quietly.

'You've sent them to Xeriphas?' She was amazed. 'But the radiation!'

'That was millions of years ago. The atmosphere will be perfectly clear now.' If it was possible for the Doctor to sound vindictive, he did so now as he added: 'Not a very nice climate for the Master, though.'

'He'll just take off again.'

'I think,' replied the Doctor mischievously, 'that with the extra energy on board, the temporal limiter

125

will need replacing.'

'He's stuck on Xeriphas?'

'Yes,' said the Doctor, earnestly. 'And I hope it's for good.' But he couldn't quite keep the doubt from creeping into his voice.

The Doctor moved back to the co-ordinates. The TARDIS was now cleared for take-off. But there was no stewardess on board.

'Where's Tegan?' he asked.

Tegan rushed through the teeming crowds of Terminal Three. It was now or never. 'I hate farewells.' Those were the Doctor's own words. She looked at the departure board. Singapore, New York, Cape Town, Honolulu … Like the voice of conscience, the tannoy burst into life. 'Departure to Sydney, Australia. Flight 342 …' She tried not to be sentimental. She had a career to think of, an exciting future with the airline. The sky was the limit … Well, Brisbane, anyway.

The debriefing in the Controller's office was not going well. At least, it was not going well for Douglas Sheard.

'The airline, not to mention Whitehall, will need some explanation for the loss of Golf Victor Foxtrot.' He was not used to having to speak so severely to senior operational staff. But the three crew members smiled patronisingly at him.

'We've rescued the passengers and crew.'

'And got our own aircraft back from a time warp.'

Shears fumed. 'A time warp indeed!'

'The Doctor was absolutely right. We've been away for three hundred million years.'

Sheard choked back his anger. Their insolence was

insupportable. 'You were only missing for ten minutes,' he retorted.

Roger Scobie gave a cry of dismay. 'What about the overtime!'

'What about Victor Foxtrot!' shouted the Controller.

'Victor Foxtrot was never really lost. Should be on the other side of the sewage farm ...'

The Controller was saved from a thrombosis by a phone call from Security.

'Not that police box again!' he protested.

The police box had indeed returned, and with it an extremely suspicious-looking young man.

'Really, officer,' the Doctor blustered to the constable, 'we're just in transit, as it were ...'

'You're amazing, Doctor!'

The Doctor, glad of the interruption, looked up to see Stapley, Bilton and Scobie approaching, in the company of a very short-tempered Airport Controller.

'Now just a moment, sir!' The constable, whatever the reason for its coming and going, was not having an unauthorised police box on his patch.

'You know my friend the Controller,' said the Doctor quickly. 'I'm sure he can give you a full-explanation.' The Doctor smiled disarmingly. 'I'll just make a quick telephone call ...' He shuffled towards the TARDIS. That'll clear the whole thing up.' He dodged inside and slammed the door.

'That police box,' said Captain Stapley to Sheard, 'is really a spaceship in disguise.'

Sheard took a sharp intake of breath.

'It's called the TARDIS,' chipped in Andrew.

'TARDIS? TARDIS?' snarled Sheard.

'Travels in time as well,' added Roger Scobie, not wanting to be left out.

Sheard decided the joke had gone far enough. 'Gentlemen,' he announced. 'If you persist with this flippancy, it will be time to talk of disciplinary action.' He looked round. There was the most peculiar noise. Not an engine the Controller had ever heard before. Something was very odd. That police box was growing paler.

And so did Douglas Sheard; because the police box … disappeared.

'Happy landings, Doctor.' Captain Stapley raised his arm in an affectionate salute.

'Happy landings,' said a plaintive voice at his elbow. Tegan looked at the empty space and a tear ran down her cheek. How she wished she hadn't dithered in the Terminal building.

'Hello,' said the Captain. 'I thought you were going with the Doctor.'

'So did I,' said Tegan.